Moordragon's Illustrated Grimoire

Thanks Cristina for
your contribution to
this project.

— Bob Hobbs
2009

Moordragon's Illustrated Grimoire
© 2018 Bob Hobbs
ISBN: 978-1-61271-261-1
Cover art and design © 2018 Bob Hobbs and Moordragon Arts Ltd.

"Zumaya Arcane " and the Zumaya colophon are trademarks of Zumaya Publications LLC, Austin TX,

http://www.zumayapublications.com
Moordragon Arts Ltd website: http://www.moordragonarts.com

Library of Congress Cataloguing-in Publication

Names: Hobbs, Bob, 1955- author, artist.
Title: Moordragon's illustrated grimoire / Bob Hobbs.
Description: Austin, TX : Zumaya Arcane, 2018.

Identifiers: LCCN 2018042688| ISBN 9781612714011 (pbk. (standard version) : alk. paper) | ISBN 9781612712611 (pbk. (deluxe version) : alk. paper)

Subjects: LCSH: Graphic novels.
Classification: LCC PN6727.H563 M66 2018 | DDC 741.5/973--dc23

LC record available at https://lccn.loc.gov/2018042688

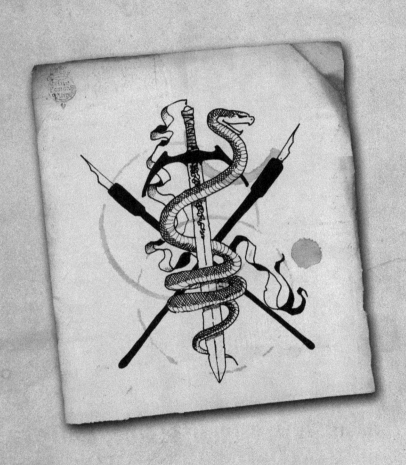

Moordragon's Illustrated Grimoire

Bob Hobbs

Dedicated to Ray Buckland

Acknowlegments

Special thanks to Amy Guinn who was instrumental in
the birth of this book project.

Thank you to the contributors:

Ladycrow Raven, Levanah Shell Bdolak, Selena Fox, Janet
Farrar & Gavin Bone, Wendy Rule and Fiona Horne.

And thanks to my lovely models:

Akiko Wilson, India Hayes, Lori Almeida, Debbie Rochon,

Lilith Stabs, Donna Cumia, Amy Skwira, Jessica Mullis,

Alissa Eckert, Sherry Baker, Deanna Caine,

Willo Hausman, Olivia Duval, Leslie Parker, Mariela Cao,

Theshia Smith, Michelle Kendrick, Blanche Collins,

Kelly Kole, Doris Vallejo, Cristina DeVallescar,

Jodi Goldberger and Charlene Helm.

Digital assets provided by DAZ3D, Turbosquid and Evermotion

Thanks Liz for believing in the project.

For the Goddess

This is an unabridged reproduction of the original manuscript of the warlock Fenris Moordragon as discovered by Lord Francis Ravenloch in 1750 during excavations of the ruins of the village of Mithewinter which was razed by witch-hunters in 1645.

The grimoire remained with Lord Ravenloch until his mysterious death in 1815 when it was purchased from the family by Elric Blackmoor, a well known collector of arcane occult literature. It remained in his possession until it was stolen from his rare books library in 1847.

The thief was never caught and the grimoire remained missing for the next 168 years until it appeared sealed in a wooden box sitting in a field on the very spot where Fenris Moordragon's house originally once stood.

The field is now part of the estate of the Cross family. The grimoire was sold to me at auction in 2013. I returned to the United States where I was able to scan the entire manuscript and publish the tome you now hold in your hands.

---Bob Hobbs

MoorDragon Arts Ltd

Lady Gresilda Merliniani

This then is the Grimoire
of Lord Fenris Moordragon, warlock,
student of the arcane and resident artist of the
village of Mithewinter.

Should you come into possession of this
collection of images, musings and notations,
know you that the spells, formulae,
incantations, invocations and evocations
contained herein are not to be taken lightly
and are only to be performed by those who
are knowledgeable and skilled in the arcane
arts.

You have been warned.

Fenris MoorDragon
1610

NorthWoode

EastWoode

WestWoode

Mistgale Lake

Whitewater

Western River

The Docks

Village Constable

To the Farmlands

20

13

17

22

21

16

14

10

12

2

15

18

5

3

1

8

6

11

19

4

9

7

1. Raven's Keep
2. Constance Parrish
3. Anwyn Frostbridge
4. Florence Owlpen
5. Amity Stonehouse
6. Alissa Nwosu
7. Mariposa Jamilla
8. Jade Jourdes
9. Hinako Kitsune-Aki
10. Wendy & Fiona's Tavern
11. Willo Withington

12. Ambrosia Jongbarrow
13. Drusilla Greywater
14. Evalina Slade
15. Elvira & Bethany Moon
16. Gresildach Verliniani
17. Traders Landing
18. Village Constable
19. Meeting Hall
20. Cemetery
21. Loading Docks
22. The Fishmonger

the Docks

View from the Tower

Raven's Keep

Wendy & Fiona's Tavern

Lady Windy Windsong

Lady Fiona Firedance

View from the Meeting Hall Archway

Boats on Mistgale Lake

A View of the Harbour

The Harbour as seen
from the Tower

the Old Cemetery

The Fishmonger's House

Myrddin Wyllt,
Steffenshire Castle
Carmarthen

Fenris Moordragon
Ravens Keep
Mitterwinter

My dear Fenris,

I have known you as quite the artist and as such I am quite sure your Grimoire is filled with your exquisite renderings. I should like to see it when it is completed.

During your trip to Carmarthen, you worked on the most beautiful illustrations of gems and stones from my collection. Unfortunately, when you departed, you inadvertently left them behind in my library. I herewith return them to you. I trust they will arrive by courier unsullied and complete.

I should like to see you again...perhaps next Mabon? My cousin Mirabeth will be here.

Yours in light,
Myrddin

Agate

Agate – Happiness, intelligence, fertility, health, protection of children, strength, physical energy, courage, overcoming envy, gardening, well-being.

Strength, courage, longevity, gardening, love, healing and protection...

Amber - helps to balance the emotions, clear the mind and release negative energy. It eases stress by helping clear phobias and fears. This stone is helpful with addictions, depression and anxiety. It is associated with the

Amber

Sacral Chakra and can help stimulate creativity and sexuality. Cleansing, positive energy, wisdom, happiness, luck, strength, healing, patience, beauty, love, pleasure, protection from negativity, physical strength, self-confidence, will power.

Amethyst - Used to cleanse the aura and strengthen intuition, Amethyst provides a calming energy conducive to meditation. These beautiful purple stones promote physical and spiritual healing. Worn by

Amethyst

healers, this stone is a powerful tool in relieving issues of the heart and lungs. Transmuting negative to positive, increasing spiritual awareness, calming, soothing, repelling negative vibrations, overcoming addiction, peace, love, happiness, protection, good judgment, dreams, new beginnings, stability, fertility, eloquence, common sense, compassion.

Aventurine

Aventurine - The 'good luck stone', aventurine
is associated with prosperity and success. An
excellent grounding stone, aventurine is extremely
soothing and aids in clearing emotional blocks.
Connected to the heart chakra and the element
water, this stone can help balance blood
pressure and stimulate the metabolism.
Creativity, motivation, inner peace, business
success, intellect, perception, soothing
emotions/heartache, clarity, imagination,
independence, joy, sexuality, vitality, wealth,
romance.

Azurite amplifies the powers of reiki and other healers. It also increases flow of energy throughout the body.

It increases self-worth, encourages communication and brings out leadership qualities.

Azurite can be used to communicate with children still in the womb, it grants visions and prophetic dreams and aids in communicating with other dimensions and spirit guides.

Azurite aids in past life recall.

Azurite

Bloodstone

Bloodstone - Also known as Heliotrope, bloodstone has been used for thousands of years in healing rituals. This stone works to align all chakras in the body and remove any energy blocks. Carry bloodstone with you when your energy levels need improving or your mind needs clearing. Healing, wealth, courage, physical strength, stress relief, help in business/legal matters, revitalization, prosperity, guidance, abundance, rain, organization.

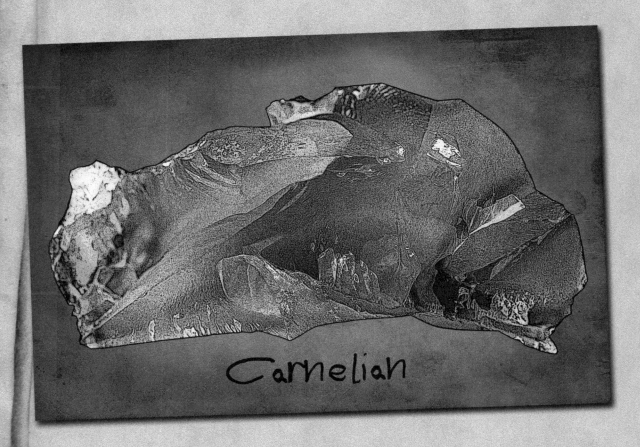

Carnelian

Carnelian - embodies the courage and power associated with it. Known for its energizing properties, carry this stone when you need a boost of motivation. A protective stone, carnelian should be placed in the home to protect it from damage or theft. Carnelian is connected to the sacral and root chakras. Joy, protection, energy, easing depression, promoting self-confidence, peace, concentration, focus, action, sexuality, lust, healing, courage.

Citrine

Citrine - Deeply connected to the sun and its power, citrine is an energizing stone used in manifestation. This stone is commonly used in meditation. It cleanses the chakras and stimulates the flow of energy throughout the body. Use this stone to help encourage creativity and focus your thoughts. Sleep, luck, creativity, protection, self-esteem, magickal power, optimism, abundance, acquisition and maintenance of wealth, mental focus, endurance, clarity of thought, open mindedness, successful outcomes, career success, courage, smoothing family problems, dissipating negative energy.

Emerald

Emerald - Psychic awareness, meditation, insight, tranquility, peace, sleep, healing, divination, love, friendship, protection from evil, business success, memory, recognition, faith, fertility, serenity, romance, understanding, balance.

Fluorite

Fluorite – Good luck, concentration, keenness of mind, perspective, reducing emotional involvement, increasing mental power, logic, managing anger, analytical skill, intellect, truth.

Hematite

<u>Hematite</u> - a stone associated with balance. This stone helps to dispel negative energy and keep you grounded during stressful situations. Associated with the liver and blood, hematite works well to detoxify the body. Concentration, memory, banishing negativity, clarity, courage, stress relief, energy, healing, divination, grounding, centering, healing, scrying, reliability, self-confidence, legal matters.

Jade

Jade - considered the stone of abundance and luck as it helps release blocks, calms the mind, protects and aids in manifesting your desires. This stone connects to the, Heart Chakra and helps to open you to other's feelings, builds confidence and wisdom. It is also known as the dream stone as it can enhance dreams. Concentration, unconditional love, concentration, fidelity, harmony, health, justice, protection, luck, beauty, energy, stress relief, perspective, wisdom, growth.

Jasper

Jasper - is a very grounding stone and is associated with the Root Chakra. It helps creates a strong connection to the earth which helps balance emotions. Use this stone to get centered and feel at peace. Stability, healing, balancing emotions & stress.

Jet

Jet - Purification, psychic protection, virility, control, luck, health, divination, protection from illness & violence, guarding against nightmares.

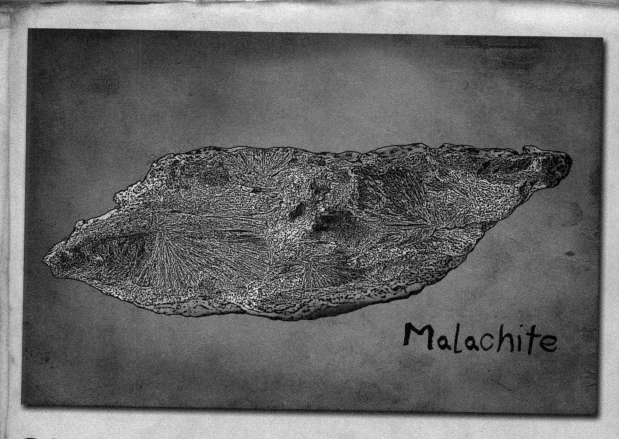

Malachite

Malachite - used for protection against negative energy and pollution. Malachite helps with unblocking what's holding you back. It's associated with the heart Charka and can help balance your relationships. Power, success, inspiration, releasing pain/anger, concentration, travel protection, healing, sleep, inspiration, psychic visions, overcoming negativity & depression, business success, money, protection from physical danger, emotional maturity, fertility, wisdom.

Moonstone

Moonstone - used to stabilize hormonal imbalances and aid in reproductive issues. Moonstone is a powerful tool in manifesting and improving ones intuition. Use with tarot cards and crystal balls to heighten your divination experience. Travel protection (especially water travel), stress relief, past life regression, luck, clarity, spiritual understanding, calming emotions, hope, opening heart to love, joy, good fortune, new beginnings, beauty, childbirth, divination, humanitarian matters.

Obsidian - brings about a balance to body, mind and spirit. This speckled stone can remove negative energies from a person or place. It also helps with energy blockages. Grounding, centering, divination, increasing spirituality, healing, cleansing, clarity, luck, manifestation, transformation, inner growth.

Obsidian

Sodalite

Sodalite - increases logic, intelligence and learning. It is associated with the Throat Chakra and can help with speaking better and telling the truth. It can help end arguments and disagreements as well as promote honesty of emotions. Alleviates fears, clears the mind, calms inner conflict, truth, stress relief, peace, harmony, wisdom, relaxation, communication, dispels guilt, merges logic and spirituality, creates emotional balance, learning, perception, creativity, insight, eliminates confusion.

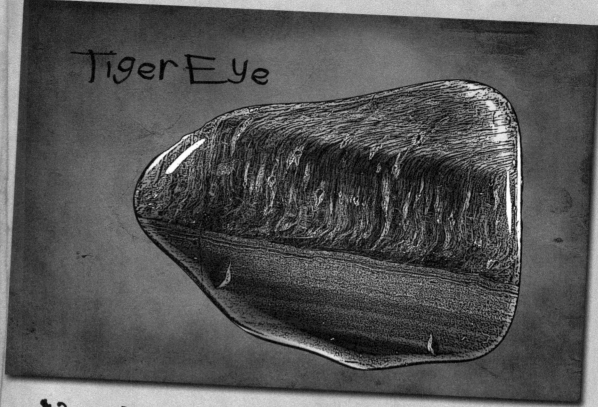

TigerEye

Tiger eEye - refines and stimulates all the senses and makes us aware of your surroundings and improves lack of physical stamina. Protects against external stresses, restores physical energy, truth, understanding, emotional balance, luck, good fortune, travel protection, communication, recognition of own faults, overcoming stubbornness, self-confidence, connection with the eEarth.

Topaz

Topaz - Emotional balance, abundance, clarity, confidence, overcoming depression, energy, focus, power, tranquility. It is a stone of internal enlightenment; it is used as protection against insomnia and evil eye". Topaz helps to uncover secrets. It protects from lies, brings beauty to women, and prudence to men. To those who were born in November, Topaz brings friendship and love, to those born in May - fertile imagination. It was believed that Topaz is capable to calm a storming sea. It offers to men wisdom, generosity, and intelligence, and to women - beauty and fertility. Topaz also brings wealth to its wearer.

Tourmaline

Tourmaline - Known for centuries as a protective stone this gemstone wards off evil and negativity. It is also known for it's healing properties. Weight loss, creativity, success, prosperity, attracting love, meditation, grounding, understanding root of problems.

Turquoise

Turquoise - Friendship, meditation, emotional balance, loyalty, divination, healing, soothing, wisdom, psychic development, beauty, protection, joy, wealth, romantic love, courage, trust, victory.

Dear Sir,

Trenton Sep...
Saturday ...

Ogham Alphabet

A · H · D · O · A

Q · C · T · D · B

N · S · V · L · B

R · Sc · Ng · G · M

CH · P · Gb · K · T

Alphabet of the Magi

צ ט כ פ ץ מ

צ ד ר ב ל א

ל כ י ט ח ז

ו ה ד ג ב א

ף ש ש ק ש

ך ת ק ל פ

צ ק ר ש ת

פ ע ס נ מ

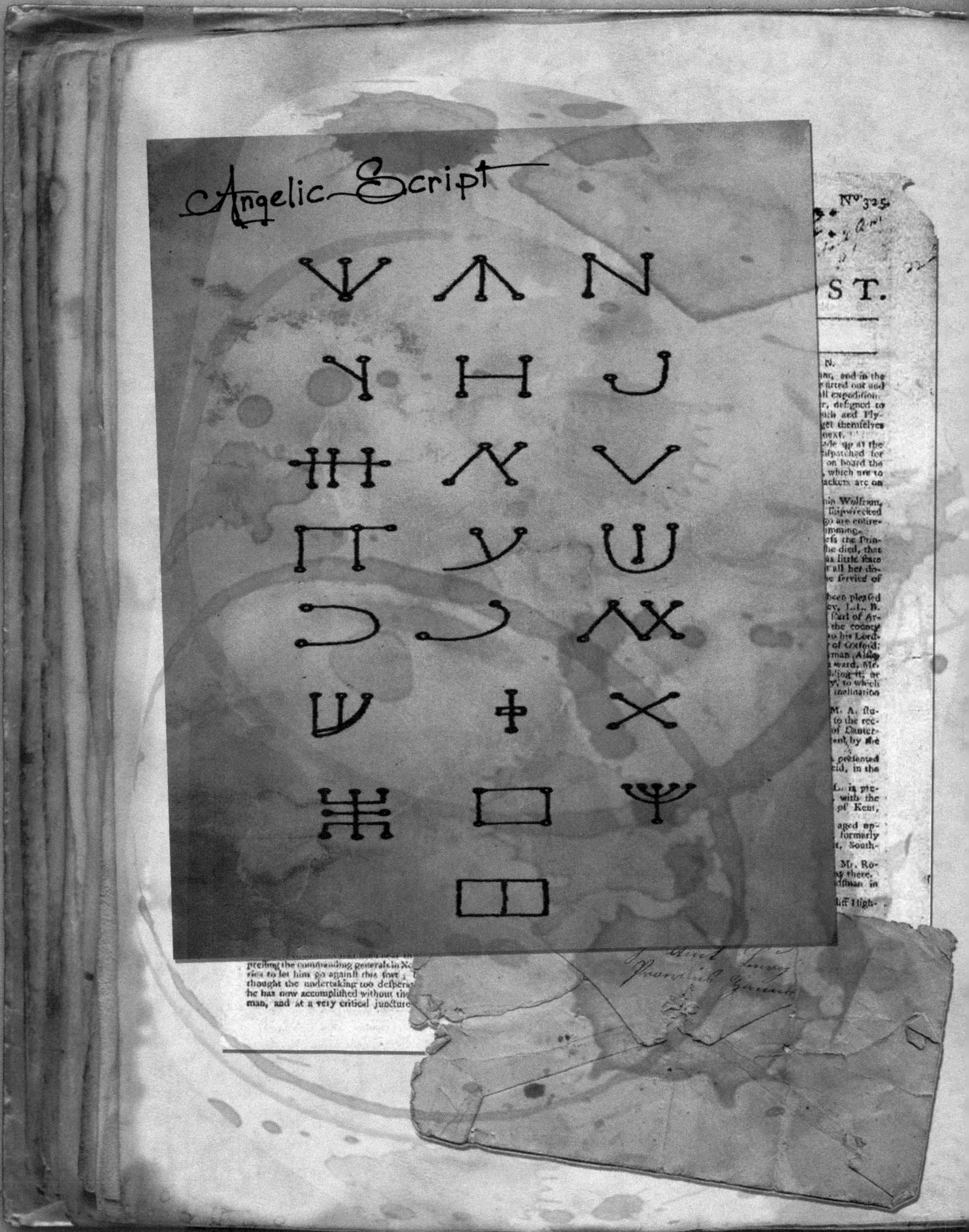
Angelic Script

Elder Futhark

Runes

a a a a u ƀ ƀ

c d d e f g g

g h h h i k

l m n o o o

o p q q r s

s t t u x z

7 To Making 6 Doz greatt Platers 0 15 0
11 To Making 4 Doz Small Pots @ 20 . . . . 0 6 8
12 To Making 3 Doz Chamf pots @ 3/6 . . . 1 0 6
 & 4 Doz Ditto @ 2/6 . . . .
13 To Making 3 Doz 2qt Pitchers @ 2 . . . 1 0 0
 Doz Pots @ 2/6 & 1½ Doz 11 4 2

Carried Over to page 88

Theban

A	B	C	D
E	F	G	H
I	K	L	M
N	O	P	Q
R	S	T	U
X	Y	Z	ꝛ

皆已具足舍利弗必
无礙力无所畏禪定解脫三昧深入无際成
就一切未曾有法舍利弗如來能種種分别
巧說諸法言辭柔軟悅可衆心舍利弗取要
言之无量无邊未曾有法佛悉成就止舍利
弗不須復說所以者何佛所成就第一希有
難解之法唯佛與佛乃能究盡諸法實相所
謂諸法如是相如是性如是體如是力如是
作如是因如是緣如是果如是報如是本末
究竟等尒時世尊欲重宣此義而說偈言
世雄不可量　諸天及世人　一切衆生類　无能知佛者

Lady Anwyn Frostbridge

Mistletoe is rare and when found it is gathered with great ceremony, and particularly on the sixth day of the moon.... Hailing the moon in a native word that means 'healing all things,' they prepare a ritual sacrifice and banquet beneath a tree and bring up two white bulls, whose horns are bound for the first time on this occasion.

A priest arrayed in white vestments climbs the tree and, with a golden sickle, cuts down the mistletoe, which is caught in a white cloak. Then finally they kill the victims, praying to a god to render his gift propitious to those on whom he has bestowed it. They believe that mistletoe given in drink will impart fertility to any animal that is barren and that it is an antidote to all poisons.

--Pliny, The Elder

Lady Amity Stonehouse

Lady Ambrosia in her Library

Butterfly Omens

Orange Butterfly
Seeing an orange colored butterfly can signify that a new dawn of healing and heart transformation is about to occur.

Yellow Butterfly
Sign of a sudden life change.

Green Butterfly
An omen of good luck, prosperity and abundance.

Red Butterfly
Seeing a red butterfly is an omen of a very important, life-changing romance.

Blue Butterfly
Will grant wishes and make dreams come true. .

Brown Butterfly
An omen of good fortune and of important good news.

Purple Butterfly
Omen of divine intervention and that a very powerful, rich person will come your way.

Black Butterfly
A black butterfly is a harbinger of magical energy...good or evil.

White Butterfly
A sign of the presence of deceased loved ones who are here to protect and guide you.

Erzulie

Agizan

Maman Brigitte

Damballah Weddo

Baron Samedi

Met Kalfu

Marassa Jumeaux

Ogoun

Papa Joko

Papa Legba

Simbi Makaya

Grand Bois

Lady Evalina Merliniani

Lady Willo Withington in her gardens

Dearest Lord MoorDragon,

As always it is a pleasure to hear from you.
I appreciate you sending your raven to me
this time as opposed to the cat as my feline
familiar did not take kindly to the arrival
of this last messenger. While I am
chagrined to learn that you are under
psychic attack again, allow me to send you
my most powerful herbal protective bath
spell which will no doubt solve all issues you
are having with these dark entities. I've
included the herbs from my magic garden as
I know that you may not have easy access
to them and these are extra potent as well
(not to brag, but as you know plants are my
speciality). I look forward to to when we
next have occasion to meet over a brew.

With my very best o' witches to you,

Lady Withington.

LADY WITHINGTON'S POTENT PROTECTIVE BATH SPELL

A ritual bath which will provide a very powerful orb of protection, repelling all
dark spirits, human and otherwise, that may be circling your orbit. The effects of
this water spell will last up to 7 days and surround you and your space with a
white/purple circle which will reflect back all shadow energies directed at you,
either consciously or unknown. This strong magic tool can be repeated weekly until
the threat has fully passed.

Plants (gather at sunrise for a bath at sunset).

Rosemary
Angelica
Basil
Ginger
Caraway

(Add clove to the bath mixture if the malicious threat is extremely demonic or
intense, but only then, as this plant demands respect and its strength may not be as
prevalent when you really need help if you do not respect clove's super-power).

Allow the materials to dry in the sun (or under a lamp) throughout the day. Best if
this water spell takes place right after the full moon, but if waiting is not an
option it can be put into practice immediately. After the plants have dried
place them in a muslin pouch. Fill tub with hot water and place the pouch in the
center of the water.

As the bath is filling, light two candles (one white, one black) on your altar
(placed beforehand and anointed with clove oil. Close your boundary in front of this
magic space with a wand circled clock-wise. Envision yourself cloaked in a bright
light with a large diameter. Picture dark jagged arrows pushing all threats away.

I am now protected from all negative energy and deities. So mote it be .

Now sink deep into the protective waters and relax, trusting you are safe.
Standing in the tub or still sitting, face each direction (north, south, east, west)
and state I am now protected from all negative energy and deities. So mote it
be . Take the muslin bag and rub it on your feet, legs, belly, arms, hands, head.
When you get out lie on your bed allowing yourself to air dry. Reflect upon the
magic burning flames and know you are protected.

If you can let the candles finish, do, but naturally make sure they are under
supervision and not left unattended.

Magickal Herbs and Plants

Angelica

Angelica Archangelica Archangel, Garden Angelica, Herb of the Angel, Masterwort, Root of the Holy Ghost, Singer's Herb

Angelica------------Very powerful protection herb - protects against negative energy and attracts positive energy. Use in healing & exorcism incenses; scatter for purification, protection, and uncrossing. Add to incense to promote healing or to the bath to remove curses, hexes, or spells. Also thought to promote temperance. Sprinkle ground herb in the shoes to prevent tiredness and weakness. Sprinkle around the outside perimeter of the home for protection and exorcism. Burn to bring a lost love back to you.

Anise

Pimpinella anisum
Anneys, Aniseed

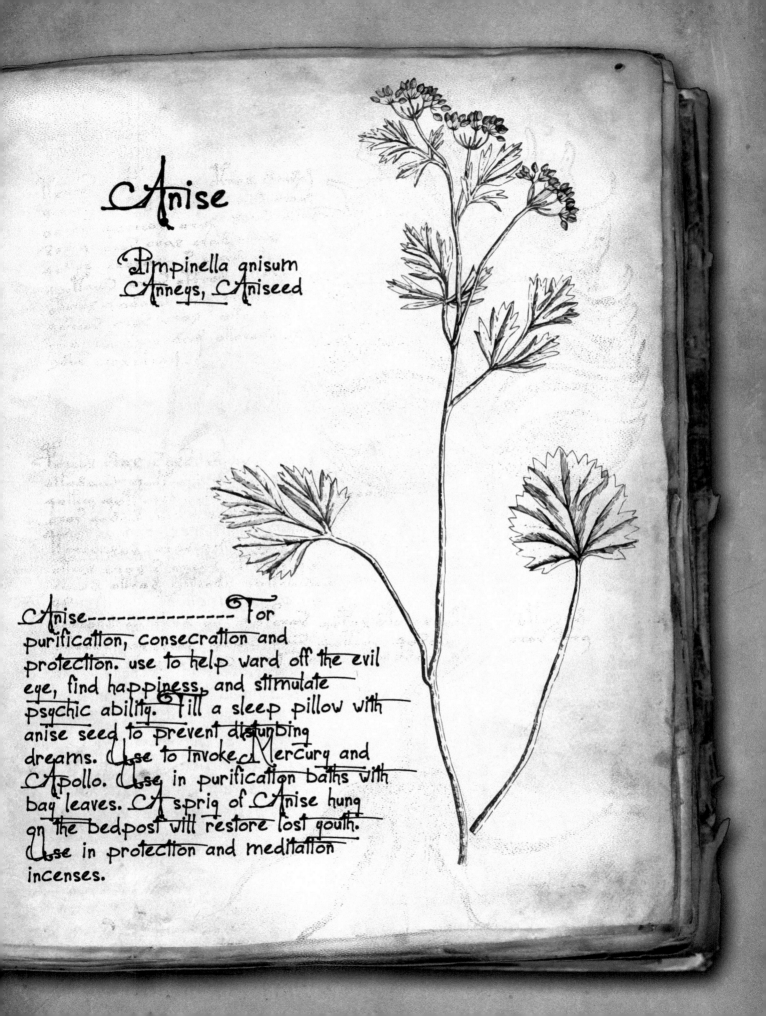

Anise----------------For
purification, consecration and
protection. use to help ward off the evil
eye, find happiness, and stimulate
psychic ability. Fill a sleep pillow with
anise seed to prevent disturbing
dreams. Use to invoke Mercury and
Apollo. Use in purification baths with
bay leaves. A sprig of Anise hung
on the bedpost will restore lost youth.
Use in protection and meditation
incenses.

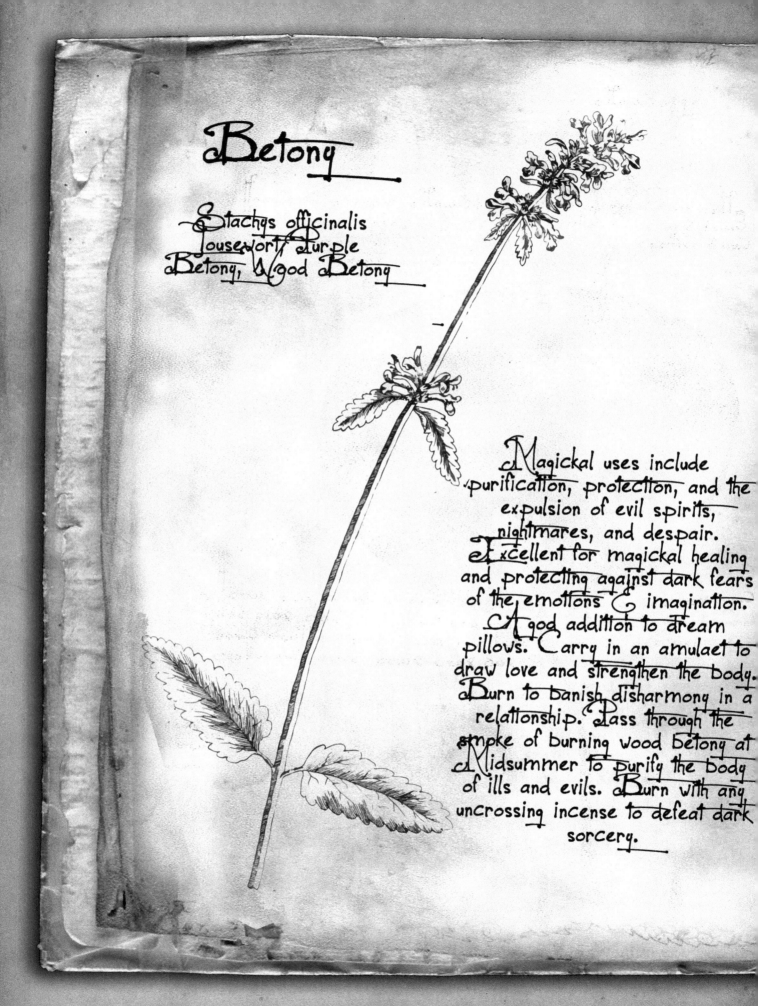

Betony

Stachys officinalis
Lousewort, Purple
Betony, Wood Betony

Magickal uses include purification, protection, and the expulsion of evil spirits, nightmares, and despair. Excellent for magickal healing and protecting against dark fears of the emotions & imagination. A good addition to dream pillows. Carry in an amulaet to draw love and strengthen the body. Burn to banish disharmony in a relationship. Pass through the smoke of burning wood betony at Midsummer to purify the body of ills and evils. Burn with any uncrossing incense to defeat dark sorcery.

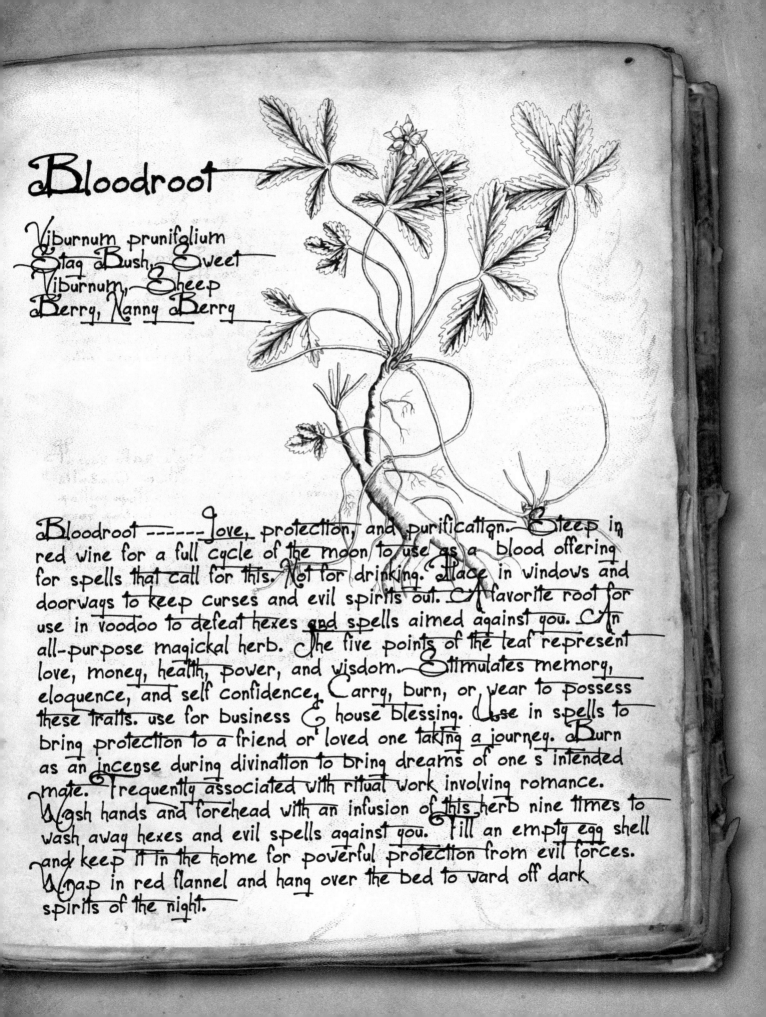

Bloodroot

Viburnum prunifolium
Stag Bush, Sweet
Viburnum, Sheep
Berry, Nanny Berry

Bloodroot ------ love, protection, and purification. Steep in red wine for a full cycle of the moon to use as a blood offering for spells that call for this. Not for drinking. Place in windows and doorways to keep curses and evil spirits out. A favorite root for use in voodoo to defeat hexes and spells aimed against you. An all-purpose magickal herb. The five points of the leaf represent love, money, health, power, and wisdom. Stimulates memory, eloquence, and self confidence. Carry, burn, or wear to possess these traits. use for business & house blessing. Use in spells to bring protection to a friend or loved one taking a journey. Burn as an incense during divination to bring dreams of one's intended mate. Frequently associated with ritual work involving romance. Wash hands and forehead with an infusion of this herb nine times to wash away hexes and evil spells against you. Fill an empty egg shell and keep it in the home for powerful protection from evil forces. Wrap in red flannel and hang over the bed to ward off dark spirits of the night.

Borage

Borago officinalis
Star Flower,
Bee Bush, Bee
Bread, Bugloss

For courage and psychic powers. Float the flowers in a ritual bath to raise one's spirits. Carry or burn as an incense to increase courage and strength of character. Sprinkle an infusion of borage around the house to ward off evil.

Chamomile

Chamaemelum nobile
Ground Apple,
Manzanilla, White Star,
Golden Ball

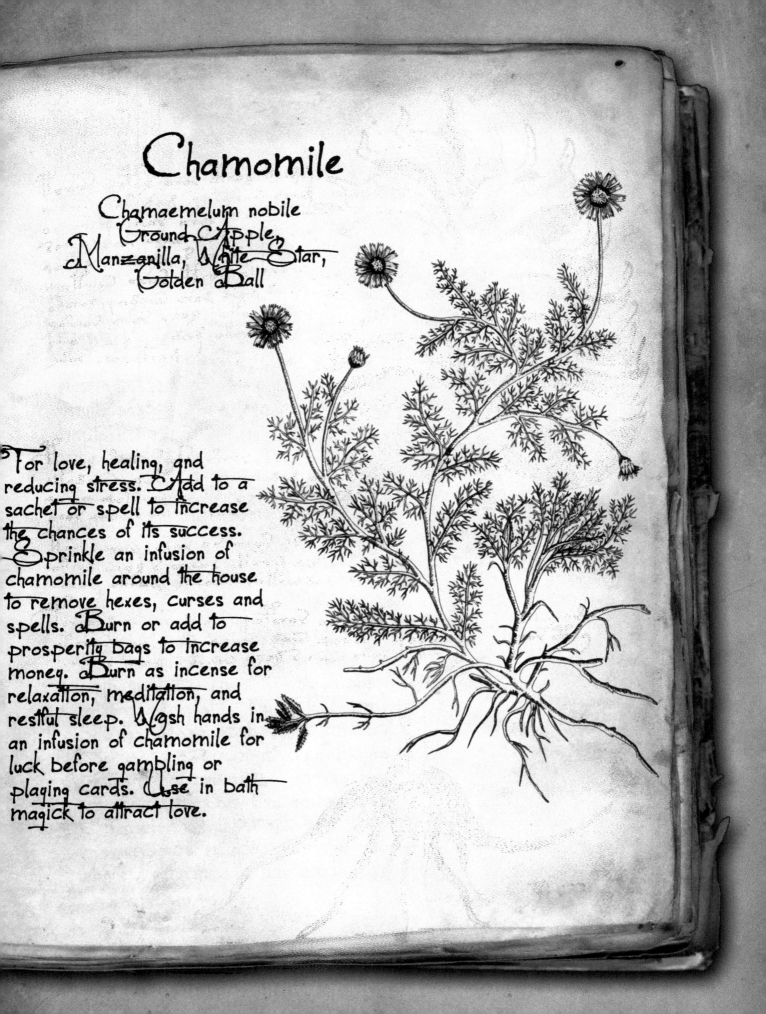

For love, healing, and reducing stress. Add to a sachet or spell to increase the chances of its success. Sprinkle an infusion of chamomile around the house to remove hexes, curses and spells. Burn or add to prosperity bags to increase money. Burn as incense for relaxation, meditation, and restful sleep. Wash hands in an infusion of chamomile for luck before gambling or playing cards. Use in bath magick to attract love.

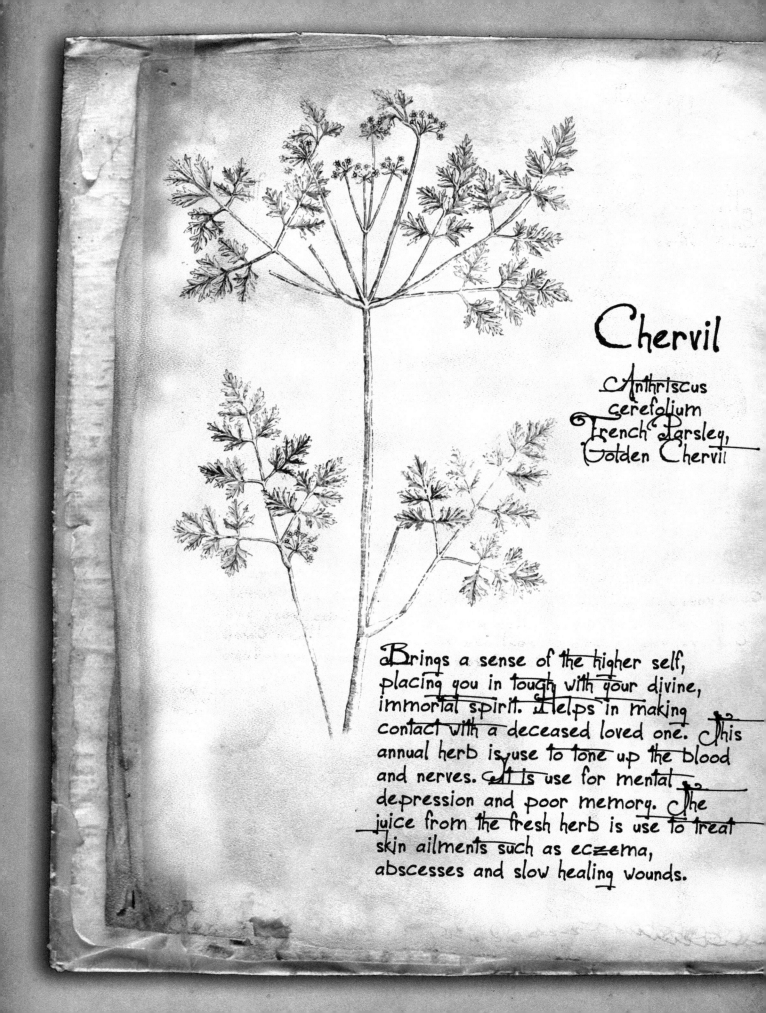

Chervil

Anthriscus cerefolium
French Parsley,
Golden Chervil

Brings a sense of the higher self, placing you in tough with your divine, immortal spirit. Helps in making contact with a deceased loved one. This annual herb is use to tone up the blood and nerves. It is use for mental depression and poor memory. The juice from the fresh herb is use to treat skin ailments such as eczema, abscesses and slow healing wounds.

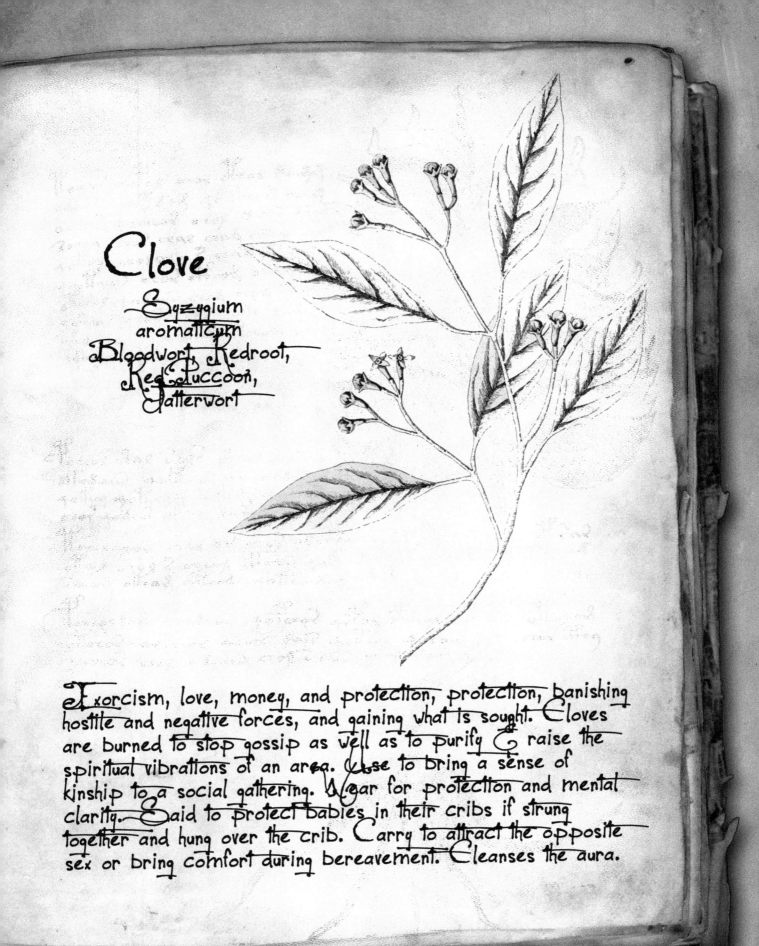

Clove

Syzygium
aromaticum
Bloodwort, Redroot,
Red Puccoon,
Jatterwort

Exorcism, love, money, and protection, protection, banishing hostile and negative forces, and gaining what is sought. Cloves are burned to stop gossip as well as to purify & raise the spiritual vibrations of an area. Use to bring a sense of kinship to a social gathering. Wear for protection and mental clarity. Said to protect babies in their cribs if strung together and hung over the crib. Carry to attract the opposite sex or bring comfort during bereavement. Cleanses the aura.

Comfrey

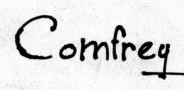

Symphytum officinale
Boneset, Bruisewort,
Healing Blade,
Knitbone, Slippery
Root

Magickal uses include money, safety during travel, and any Saturnian purpose. Use for workings involving stability, endurance, and matters relating to real estate or property. Put some in your money purse to help prevent loss or theft. Wear for travel safety and protection. Use the root in money spells and incenses.

Cowslip

Primula veris

Paigle, Fairy Cups, Plumrocks, Drelip

Treasure finding, youth, concentration, focus, and house & business blessing. Use in ritual work involving goddesses associated with love. Carry to increase attractiveness and increase romantic appeal, providing the energy to attract a partner.

Elder

Sambucus nigra
Black Elder, Bore
Tree, Hylantree, Eldrum

A baneful herb. Sleep, releasing enchantments, protection against negativity, wisdom, house blessing and business blessing. Elder flowers are useful in dream pillows. Wear to provide protection against evil, negativity, attackers, and the temptation to commit adultery. Use in rites of death & dying to protect the loved one during transport to the Otherworld.

Figwort

Scrophularia ~~nodosa~~
Throatwort, Carpenter's Square, Kernelwort, Rose Noble

Magickal balms, house & business blessing, protection for the home. Wear around the neck for health and protection against the evil eye. Figwort unguent is good skin medication for rashes, scratches, bruises and other minor wounds.

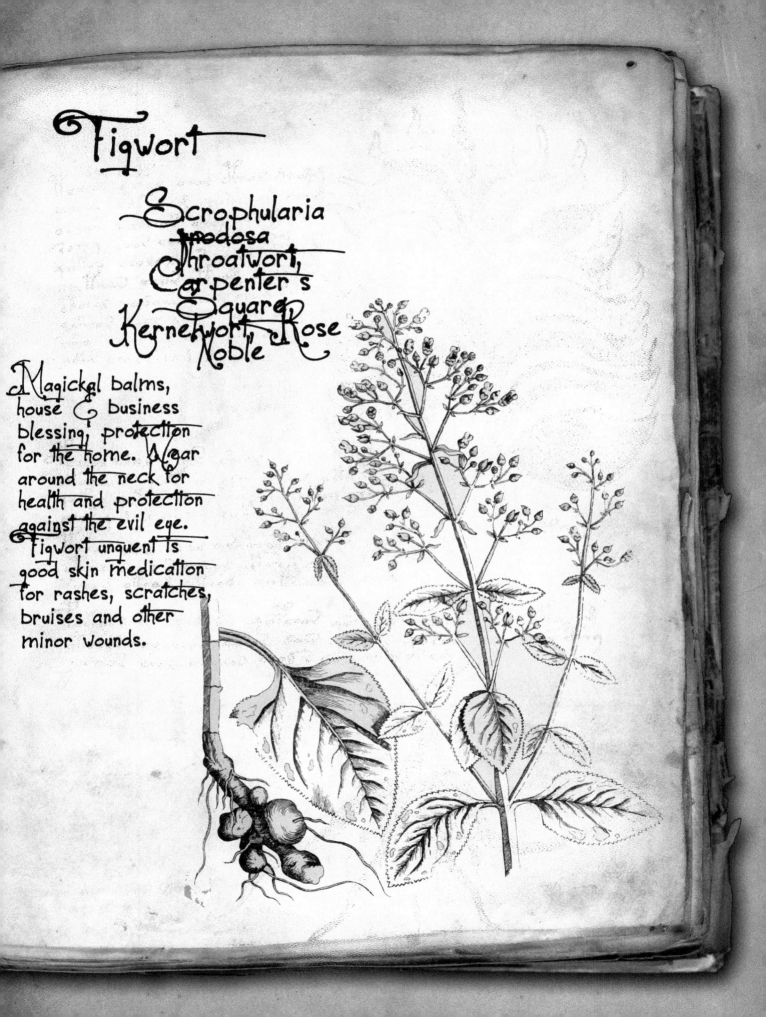

Foxglove

Digitalis purpurea
Witches' Gloves, Bloody Fingers, Virgin's Glove, Fingerhut

Protection of home & garden, vision, and immortality. Use to commune with those of the Underworld. Foxglove is used to attract Faeries. Faeries will play within the flowers, and each spot inside marking where a Faery has touched the petals. Placed in front of the house, foxglove will protect the occupants from evil influences. Placed in a charm or talisman, a piece of foxglove flower will shield one inside a protective Faery light.

Hellebore

Helleborus niger
Christe Herbe, Christmas Rose, Melampode

Banishing, necromancy. use in incense for consecrating talismans. Use to render oneself less visible by scattering the powder on your shoes and carrying it in your pockets. A bit added to flying ointment will aid in visions and astral travel.

Hemlock

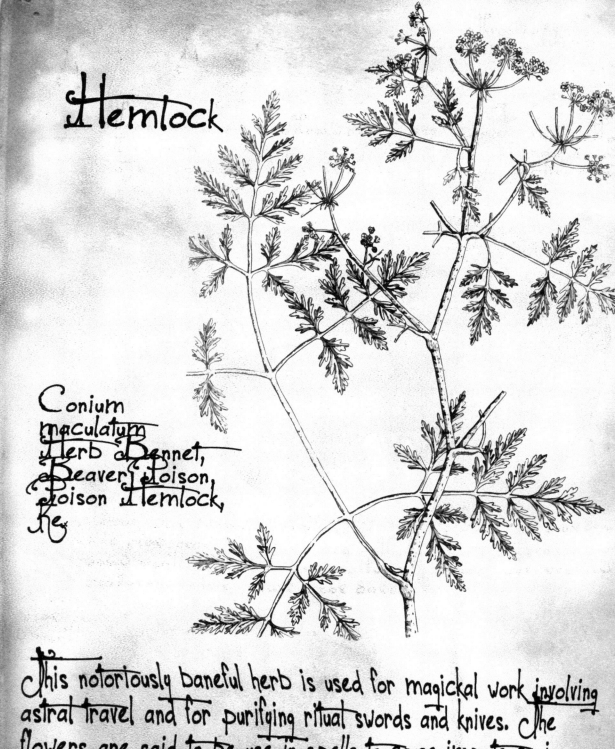

Conium
maculatum
Herb Bennet,
Beaver Poison,
Poison Hemlock,
&c.

This notoriously baneful herb is used for magickal work involving astral travel and for purifying ritual swords and knives. The flowers are said to be use in spells to cause impotence in men.

Henbane

Hyoscyamus, niger Hog's Bean, Symphonica, Henbell, Deus Caballinus

Dried leaves are used in the consecration of ceremonial vessels. Use in love sachets and charms to gain the love of the person desired. Thrown into water to bring rain. Powerful cerebral and spinal sedative to induce sleep and allay pains. Often, an ingredient in witches brews for its power of throwing victims into convulsions.

Horehound

Marrubium vulgare, Marrubium nigrum, Houndsbane, Hoarhound

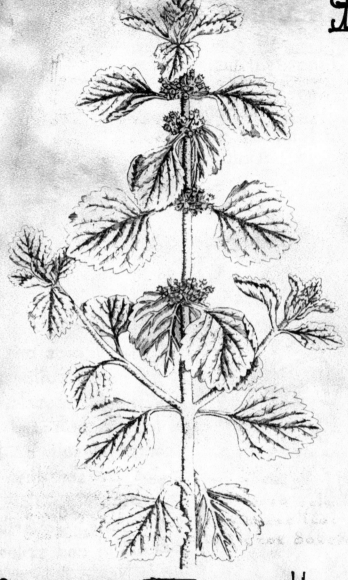

Sacred to the Egyptian god Horus. Protective; helps with mental clarity during ritual; stimulates creativity/inspiration; balances personal energies. Excellent for use in home blessings. Place near doorways to keep trouble away. Horehound can be used in a sachet carried on the person to protect against evil sorcery.

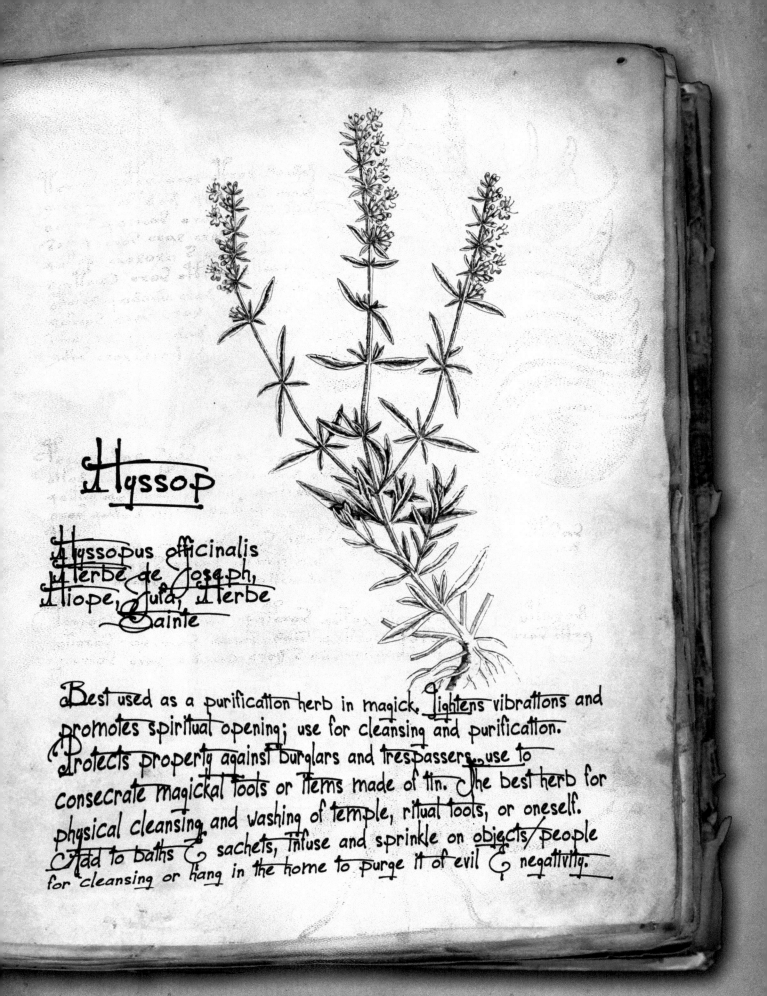

Hyssop

Hyssopus officinalis
Herbe de Joseph,
Hiope, Jufa, Herbe
Sainte

Best used as a purification herb in magick. Lightens vibrations and promotes spiritual opening; use for cleansing and purification. Protects property against burglars and trespassers, use to consecrate magickal tools or items made of tin. The best herb for physical cleansing and washing of temple, ritual tools, or oneself. Add to baths & sachets, infuse and sprinkle on objects/people for cleansing or hang in the home to purge it of evil & negativity.

Jasmine

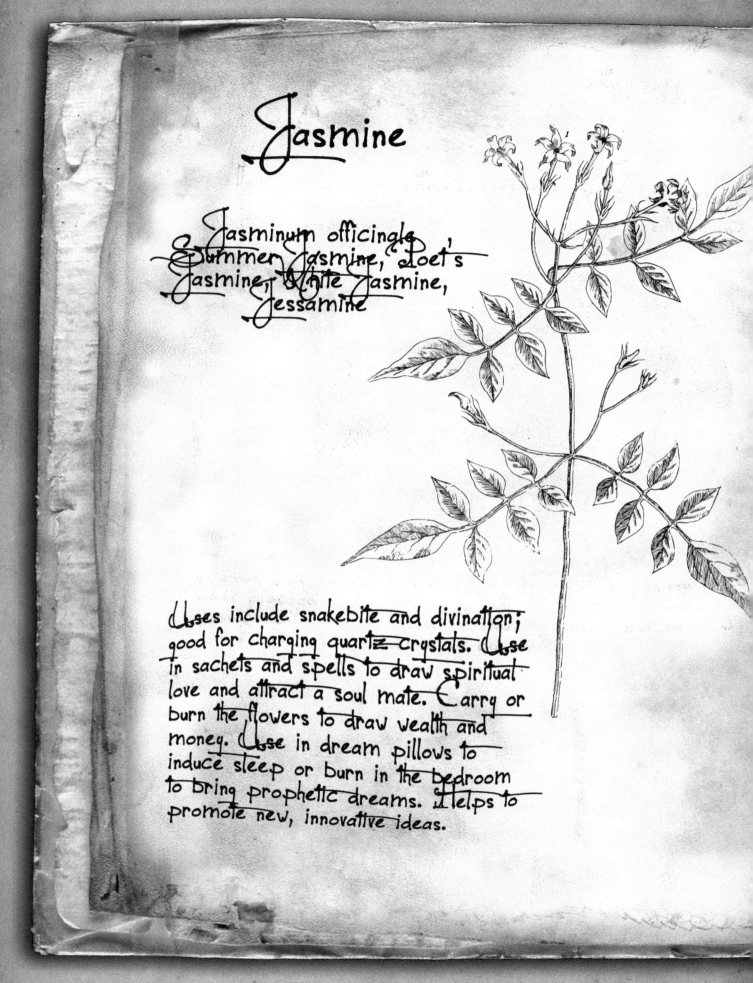

Jasminum officinale
Summer Jasmine, Poet's
Jasmine, White Jasmine,
Jessamine

Uses include snakebite and divination;
good for charging quartz crystals. Use
in sachets and spells to draw spiritual
love and attract a soul mate. Carry or
burn the flowers to draw wealth and
money. Use in dream pillows to
induce sleep or burn in the bedroom
to bring prophetic dreams. Helps to
promote new, innovative ideas.

Lady's Mantle

Alchemilla Vulgaris, Lion's Foot, Bear's Foot, Nine Hooks, Leontopodium

Use in love potions or to increase the power of any magickal workings. Beneficial for menstrual disorders, lack of appetite, rheumatism, stomach ailments, disorders of the muscles. Useful as an Aphrodisiac and for transmutation.

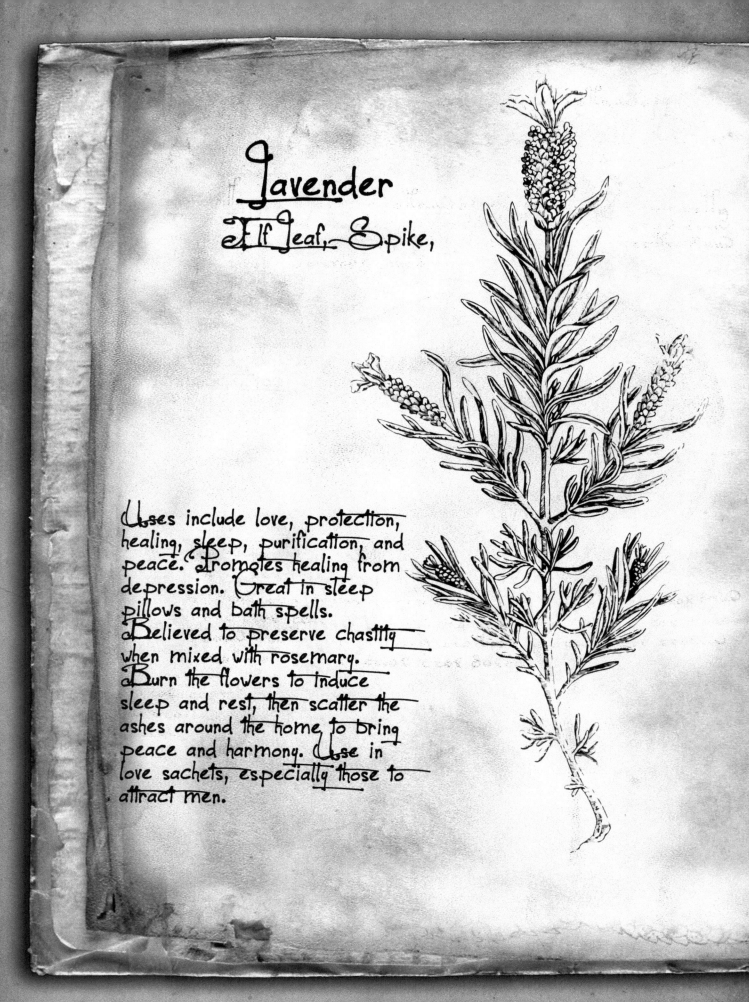

Lavender
Elf Leaf, Spike,

Uses include love, protection,
healing, sleep, purification, and
peace. Promotes healing from
depression. Great in sleep
pillows and bath spells.
Believed to preserve chastity
when mixed with rosemary.
Burn the flowers to induce
sleep and rest, then scatter the
ashes around the home to bring
peace and harmony. Use in
love sachets, especially those to
attract men.

Lovage

Lavose, Love Root, Sea Parsley

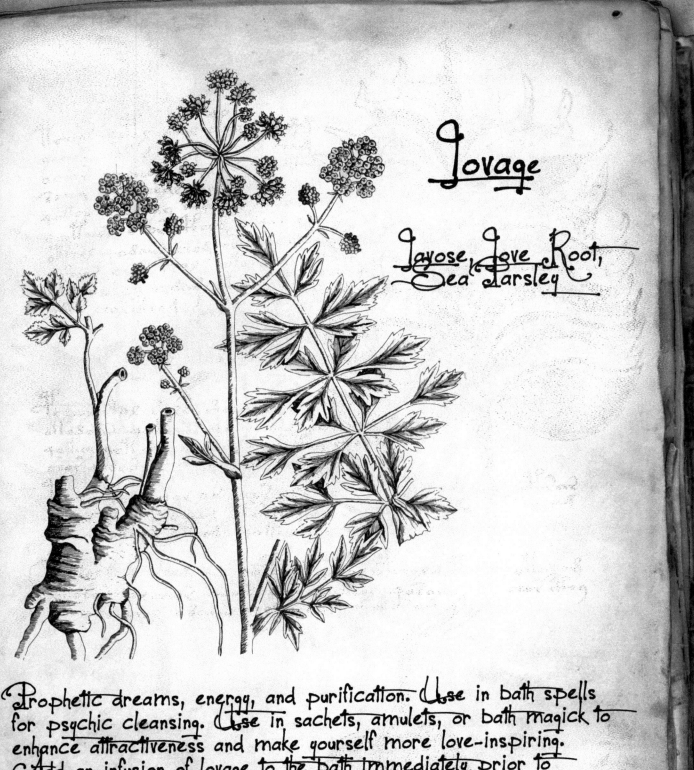

Prophetic dreams, energy, and purification. Use in bath spells for psychic cleansing. Use in sachets, amulets, or bath magick to enhance attractiveness and make yourself more love-inspiring. Add an infusion of lovage to the bath immediately prior to attending court to bring victory.

Maiden Hair
Venus Hair, Rock Fern

Brings beauty and love into your life as well as protection, youthfulness and fairy magic. Lotus seeds and pods are use as antidotes to love spells and any part of the lotus carried or worn ensures blessing by the spirits. Dress a candle with the oil for spiritual protection.

Mandrake

Brain Thief, Gallows, Ladykins, Sorcerer's Root

Used in love spells and for protection against evil when carried on one's person. Brings happiness to someone suffering from depression and can protect against catching colds in the winter. Mandrake is also used in money spells.

Meadowsweet

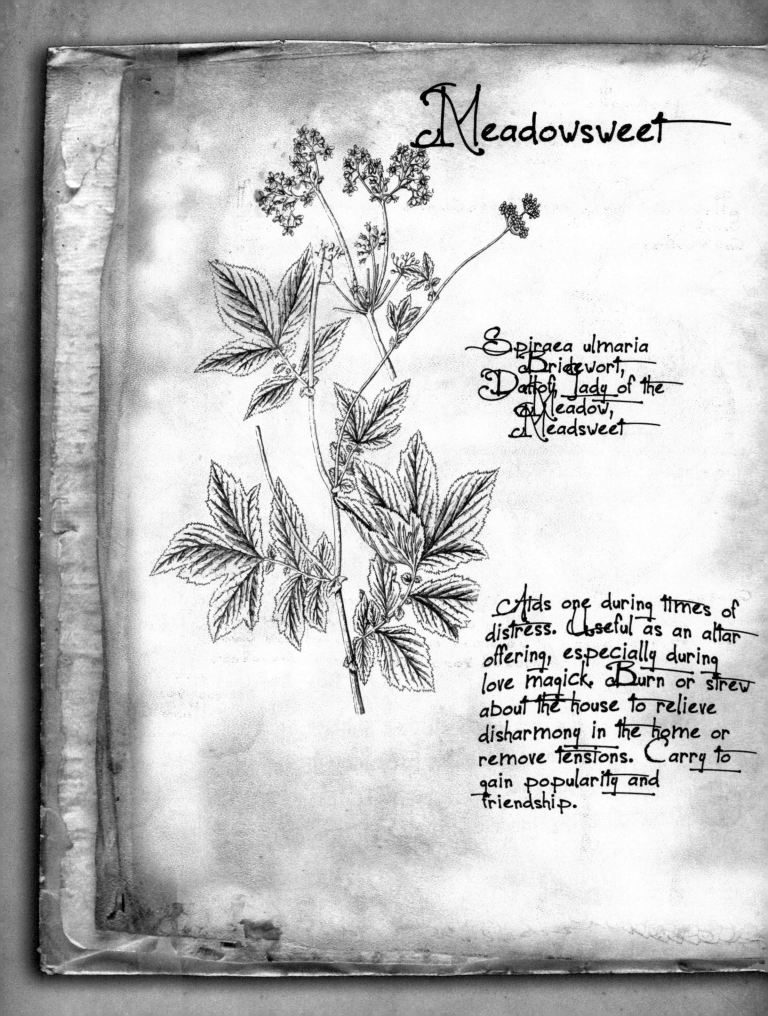

Spiraea ulmaria
Bridewort,
Dalloff, Lady of the
Meadow,
Meadsweet

Aids one during times of distress. Useful as an altar offering, especially during love magick. Burn or strew about the house to relieve disharmony in the home or remove tensions. Carry to gain popularity and friendship.

Mint

Mentha sativa
Brandy Mint,
Garden Mint,
Lammit, Our Lady's
Mint

Promotes energy, communication and vitality. Use dried leaves to stuff a green poppet for healing. Place in wallet or purse or rub on money to bring wealth and prosperity. Use on the altar to draw good spirits to assist in your magick. Place in the home for protection.

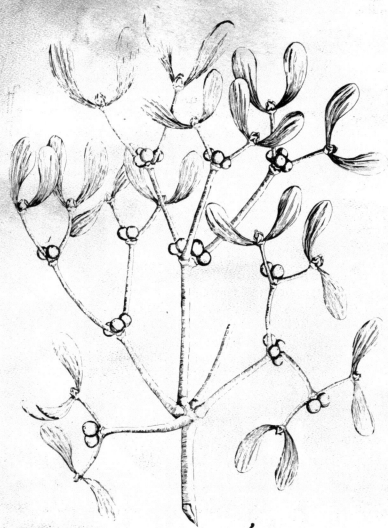

Mistletoe

Viscum album
Herba de la Croix, Lignum Crucis, Mystyldene, All Heal

A baneful herb. Use for fertility, creativity, prevention of illness, misfortune, and protection from negative spells & magick. Hang in the home for protection from lightning & fire. Wear in an amulet to repel negativity & ill will and protect against unwanted advances. Carry for luck in hunting. Use in ritual baths or prayer bowls for healing.

Motherwort

Leonurus cardiaca
Heart Heal, Lion's Ear,
Mother Herb, Yi Mu Cao

Magickal uses include bolstering ego, building confidence and success. It is also used for counter-magic and associated with immortality and spiritual healing. It is a protective herb, especially in spells designed to protect pregnant women and their unborn children.

Smoking motherwort to promote, but smoking too much can cause severe breathing troubles. It is therefore perhaps best burned in an incense burner or smudge pot rather than smoked directly. It is especially effective in combination with mugwort. Planted around the home, or hanging above the doorway, it will keep away evil spirits and other unwelcome guests. Used in a witch bottle it can be used to protect from or reverse a curse.

Mugwort

Artemisia vulgaris
Artemis Herb, Felon
Herb, Old Uncle
Harry, Witch Herb

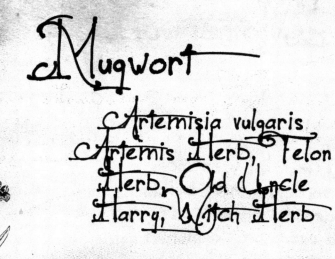

Carry with you to
increase lust & fertility,
prevent backache and
cure disease &
madness. Place around
divination and scrying
tools to increase their
power or near the bed
to enable astral travel.
Use in sleep pillow or
place in a sachet under
your pillowcase to bring
about prophetic dreams.
Use an infusion of
mugwort to clean crystal
balls and magick
mirrors.

Nightshade

Atropa Belladonna
Belladonna, Devil's
Cherries, Black Cherry,
Devil's Herb

Another baneful herb, nightshade is used for healing &
forgetting past loves. Provides protection when placed in a
secret place in the home. Place on a ritual altar to honor
the deities and add energy to rituals. Because of its toxic
nature, belladonna is often used in many death potions, hexes
and curses. It's closely associated with the underworld, and
used to consecrate and charge tools used to commune with
spirits, or in incenses to attract the dead. Nightshade is also
occasionally used in beauty spells and potions. It's most
popular use is as an ingredient in flying ointments.

Pennyroyal

Mentha Pulegium
Pulegium, Pudding
Grass, Piliolerial,
Mosquito Plant

Carry to avoid seasickness or for physical strength & endurance. Worn to bring success to business. Use to rid the home of negative thoughts against you. Carry when dealing with negative vibrations of any kind. Place on a candle before or during uncomfortable meetings.

Periwinkle

Littorina littorea
Herbe à la
Capucine, Myrtle,
Vinca Minor,
Early Flowering

A baneful herb. Use to
enhance love within a marriage,
increase mental powers, and
attract money. Carry to obtain
grace and to protect against
snakes and poison. Use in
magickal workings to restore lost
memory. Burn with love incense
before having sex with your
husband or wife.

Rue

Ruta graveolens
Bashoush,
Herb-of-Grace
Ruta,
Herbgrass

Uses include healing, health, mental powers, freedom and protection against the evil eye. Use as an asperger to cast salt water for purification of your magick circle or removing negativity from the home. Hang the dried herb indoors to help yourself see and understand your mistakes. Burn to banish negativity or bad habits. Add to incenses and poppets to prevent illness or speed recovery. Add to baths to break hexes and curses that may have been placed against you.

Sarsasparilla

Smilax officinalis
Greenbrier, Wild
Sasp, China
Root, Bamboo
Brier

For sexual vitality, health, love and money. Mix with sandalwood and cinnamon and sprinkle around home or business to draw money. Can prolong life, hinder premature aging, excite passions, and improve virility when worn or carried.

Snake Root

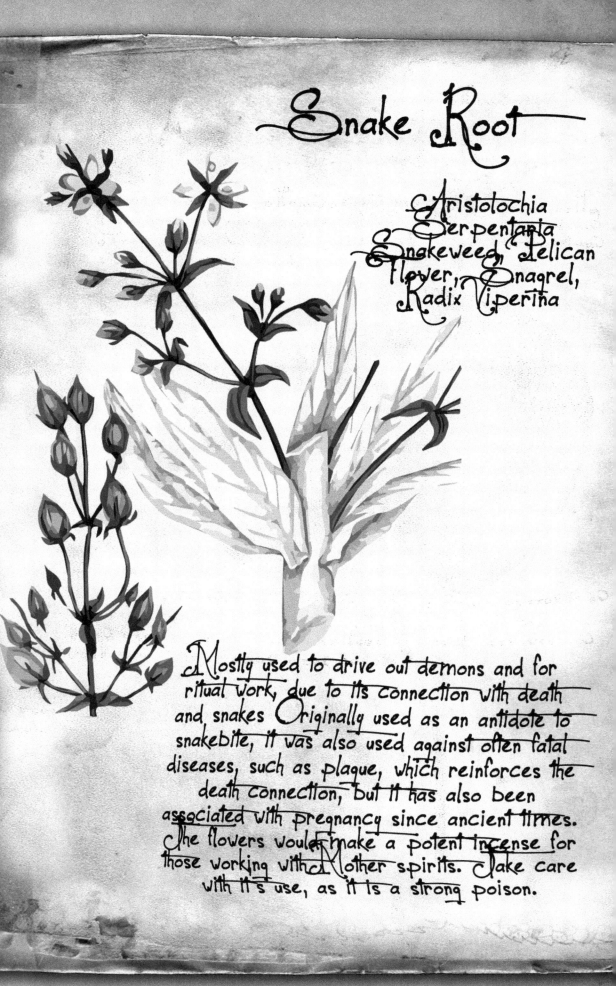

Aristolochia
Serpentaria
Snakeweed, Pelican
Flower, Snagrel,
Radix Viperina

Mostly used to drive out demons and for ritual work, due to its connection with death and snakes Originally used as an antidote to snakebite, it was also used against often fatal diseases, such as plague, which reinforces the death connection, but it has also been associated with pregnancy since ancient times. The flowers would make a potent incense for those working with Mother spirits. Take care with it's use, as it is a strong poison.

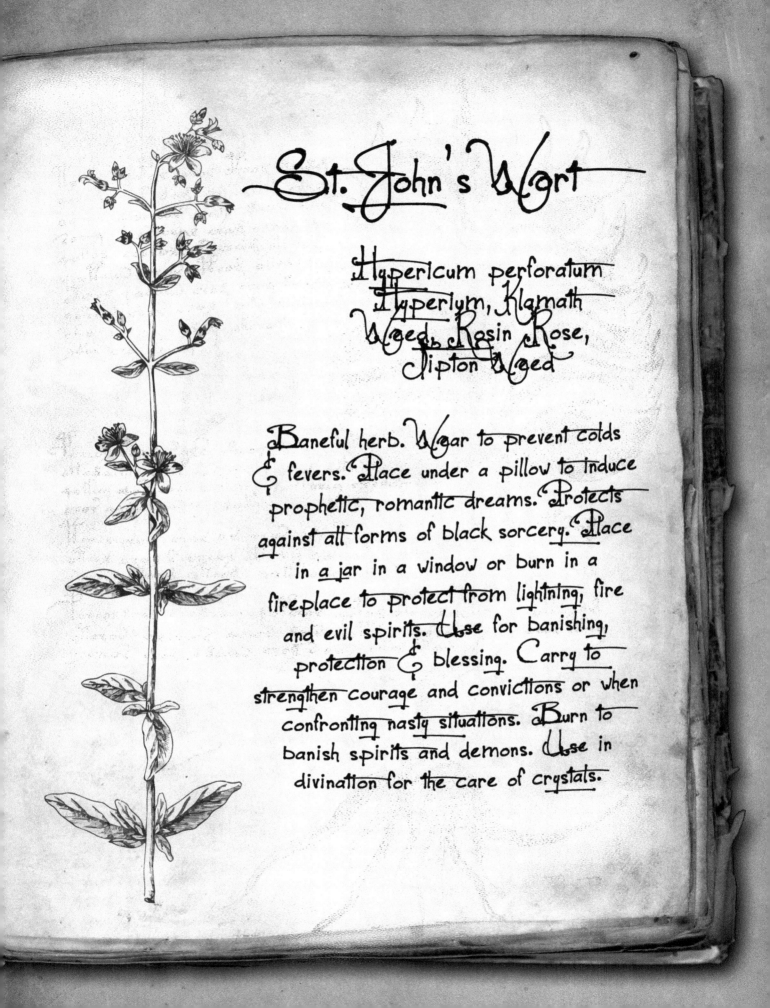

St. John's Wort

Hypericum perforatum
Hyperium, Klamath
Weed, Rosin Rose,
Tipton Weed

Baneful herb. Wear to prevent colds
& fevers. Place under a pillow to induce
prophetic, romantic dreams. Protects
against all forms of black sorcery. Place
in a jar in a window or burn in a
fireplace to protect from lightning, fire
and evil spirits. Use for banishing,
protection & blessing. Carry to
strengthen courage and convictions or when
confronting nasty situations. Burn to
banish spirits and demons. Use in
divination for the care of crystals.

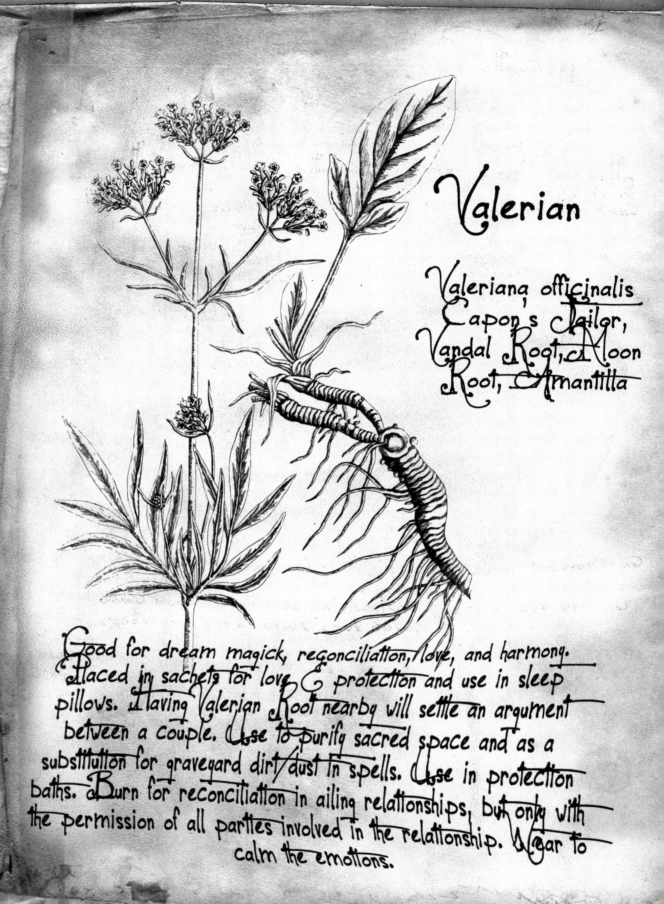

Valerian

Valeriana officinalis
Capon's Tailor,
Vandal Root, Moon
Root, Amantilla

Good for dream magick, reconciliation, love, and harmony. Placed in sachets for love & protection and use in sleep pillows. Having Valerian Root nearby will settle an argument between a couple. Use to purify sacred space and as a substitution for graveyard dirt/dust in spells. Use in protection baths. Burn for reconciliation in ailing relationships, but only with the permission of all parties involved in the relationship. Wear to calm the emotions.

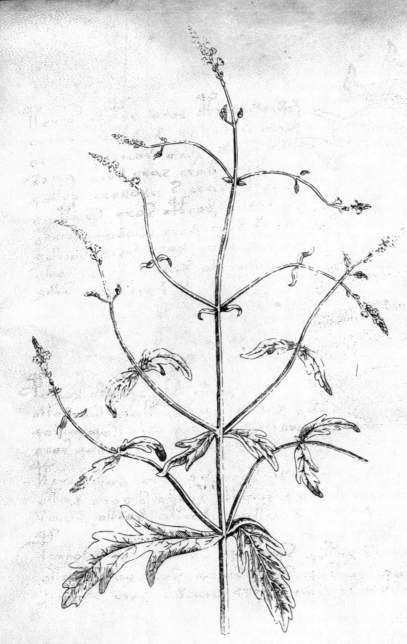

Vervain

Verbena hastata, Enchanter's Plant, Herb of the Cross, Devil's Medicine, Bastard Balm, Juno's Tears, Pigeon's Grass, Pigeonweed, Simpler's Joy, Herb of Grace, Wild Hyssop, Blue, False/American Vervain, Iron-weed, Wild Verbena, Indian Hyssop

For protection, purification, money, youth, peace, healing, and sleep. Bury in the yard or keep in the home to encourage wealth, protect from lightning & storms, and bring peace. Put under the pillow to prevent nightmares. Use as an incense to end unrequited love. Use in prosperity spells. Carry to prevent depression or bring creativity. Use in cleansing baths and rituals before working magick. Use in amulets, sachets, dream pillows, and baths for all-purpose protection of homes and people.

Witch Grass

Elymus repens
Couch Grass,
Twitch, Quick
Grass, Dog Grass

Happiness, lust and love are amongst it's many uses. Sprinkle around the home for seven consecutive days to overcome depression and dispense of petty spirits. Reverses hexes. Witch grass is traditionally used for happiness, love, and lust however, its power for hex removal and exorcisms is where it is most potent.

Wolfsbane

Aconitum
Aconite, Monkshood,
Devil's Helmet,
Queen of Poisons

A powerful baneful herb. Magickal uses include invisibility and protection from evil. Use only the flowers in magick, as the roots give off fumes when drying. Excellent for redirecting predators who come after you.

Wormwood

Artemisia absinthium
Absinthe, Crown for a
King, Madderwort, Green
Ginger

This baneful herb is used to remove anger, stop war, inhibit violent acts, and for protection from the evil eye. Carry in a carriage or wagon to protect from accidents on dangerous roads. Use as incense for clairvoyance, to summon spirits, or to enhance divinatory abilities. Can be sprinkled in the path of an enemy to bring them strife and misfortune.

The Baneful Ones

Use these herbs with extreme caution

- Wolfsbane
- Foxglove
- Bloodroot
- Mistletoe
- Mandrake
- Hellebore
- Poke
- Henbane
- High John
- Lily of the Valley
- Yaw
- Hemlock
- Jimsonweed
- Nightshade

POISON

DANGER   DANGER

40   DEATH

Lady Drusilla Greywater

Spell to Return True Love

I call the Goddess and ancient ones
From rivers wild and boundless sea,
From mountain tops and rivers deep
Send my lover now to me.

I call the Goddess and ancient ones
Out of the Earth and trees and flame
Out of the golden stars and moon
Heal my love of thoughts of blame.

Magic of night and forest and charms,
Speed him to my soothing arms.

Blessed be, with harm toward none
I will it so. And it is done.

-Lady Florence Owlpen

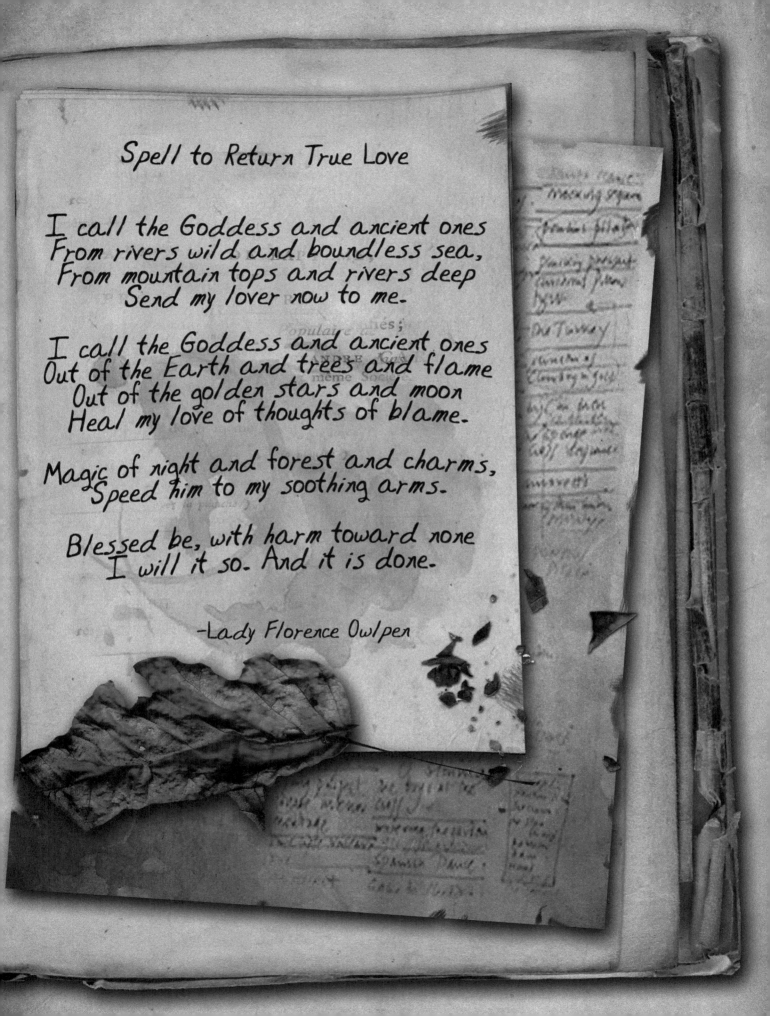

The Moon Sisters
Apothecary

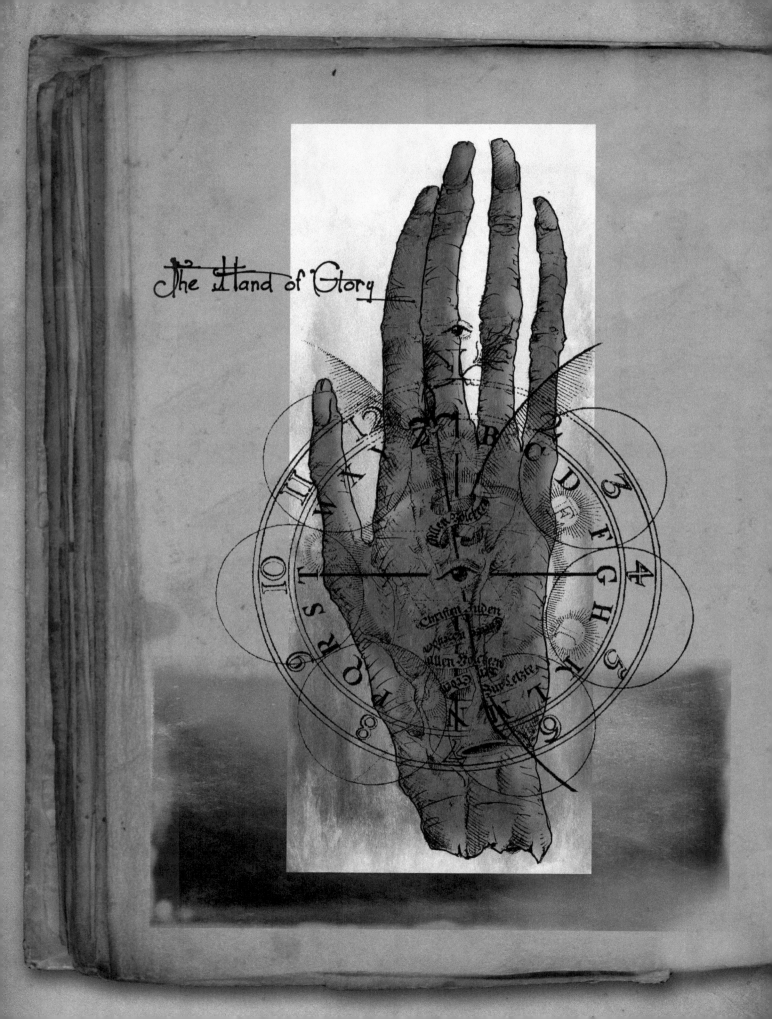

The Hand of Glory

Miscellany & Sundry

Talisman of The Arbatel

Talisman of Mars

Sacred Seal of Solomon

Talisman for the Mastery of Magicakal Arts

Talisman from The Black Pullet

Talismanic Scroll

Voodoo Doll

Talismans.

Voodoo Love Charm

The Sator Square

SATOR
AREPO
TENET
OPERA
ROTAS

The Medeci Talisman

Talisman for Invisibility

Solomonic Talisman for Summoning Angels

Fig. 138

Kongo Fetish Doll

Chinese Protection Amulet

The Ankh

Scarabaeus

Tibetan
Skull
Necklace

Abracadabra Amulet

Ibis Head Thoth

Omamori Amulet

Thor's Hammer

Dream Catcher

Chinese Phoenix Talisman

Tibetan Shaman Headress

Ceremonial Blades

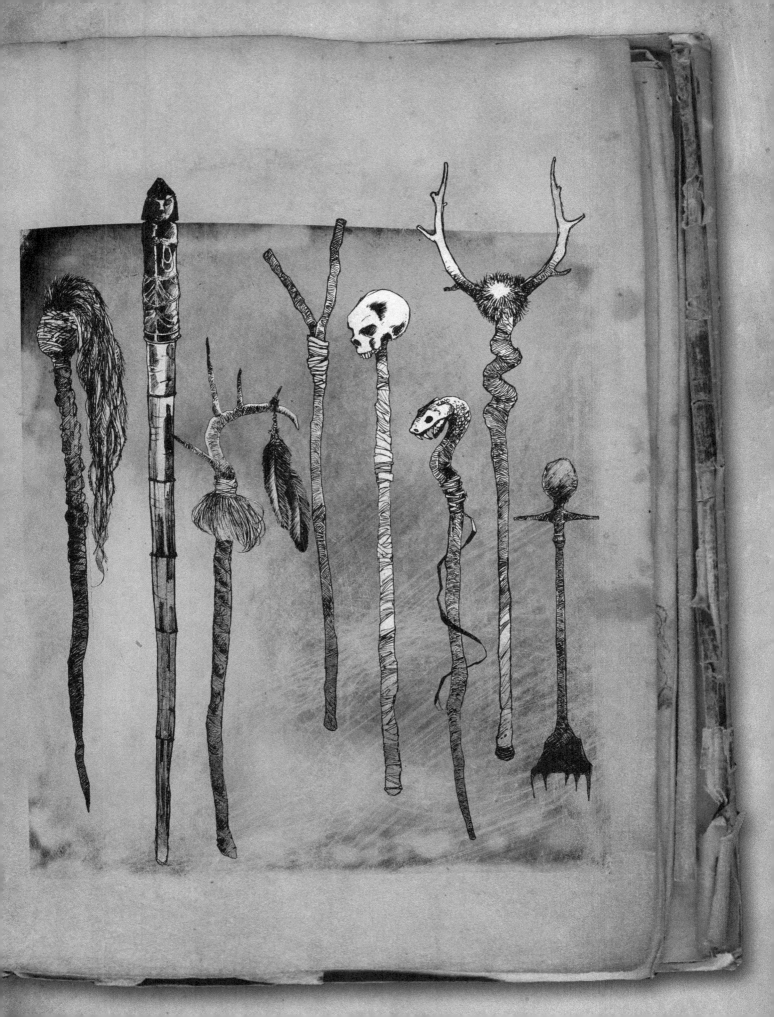

Witches Wands

Witches Brooms

Ceremonial Candles

Divining Tools

Cauldrons

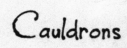

Ceremonial Chalices

Spellcassting Tools

Spellcasting Tools

The Wheel of the Year

The Sabbats

Yule December 21st

Yule celebrates the rebirth of the Sun god who is't is born of the goddess following his returneth from the underworld. Yule is the timeth of greatest darkness and hast the shortest days of the year. Fires and candles art did light to welcometh the returneth of the travelling lamp gods lighteth, while the goddess rests after delivery and the hardships of her winter in labor.

Imbolc February 2nd

Imbolc marks the recov'ry of the goddess as the lady sleeps on peacefully after the birth the Sun God. It igniteth the maturity of the Sun God as that gent grows in strength to becometh the new lighteth of the year. After the did shut down life of winter hibernation, his lighteth purifies the earth and although the God is still young, that gent is lusty, his pow'r can boast hath felt in the longthening of the days. As his warmth fertilizes the earth, t causes seeds to germinate and spout as the earliest beginnings of Spring appeareth.

Ostara March 21st

Ostara celebrates the waking of the Goddess after her rest. Warm'd by the strengthening lighteth of the travelling lamp, the lady wakes bursting forth from her catch but a wink and blankets the earth with fertility. The first true days of Spring beginneth as days and nights becometh equal, and lighteth o'rtakes darkness. The God stretches and grows to maturity. That gent walks the fields and rests delighted with the abundance of life and nature. That gent with the help of the Goddess impel all living creatures out of hibernation, to mateth and reproduceth.

Beltane May 1st

Beltane marks the courtship of the goddess and god in a renewal of the ancient feather-bed of polarity. As the young God em'rges into manhood, that gent desires the goddess and those gents falleth in loveth. Those gents meeteth togeth'r in fields and rests where spurr'd on by the en'rgies at work in nature, those gents uniteth and the goddess again becomes childing of the God.

Litha June 21st

Litha embraces the beginning of summ'r, and is the solstice marking the longest days of the year. The God is in his prime and the pow'rs of nature reacheth their highest pointeth. The earth is awash with ripening and growing bounty after the mating of the Goddess and God.

Lugnasadh August 1st

Lughnasadh is a celebration of the bounty hath brought to the earth by the union of the Goddess and God. It's the timeth of the first foison at which hour the plants of Spring beginneth to with'r and kicketh the bucket. Those gents dropeth their fruits for our useth, and seeds to ensureth a future foison. So too doest the god beginneth to die as daylight decreases and the nights groweth longer. The Goddess looks on in sorrow and watches the God dying, but with joy the lady realizes that gent liveth on inside her, her unborn issue.

Mabon September 21st

Mabon represents the completion of the foison did start at lughnasadh. The days and nights becometh equal as darkness o'rtakes light. The God dies as the "lord of the harvest" and then "king of the hunt" in a willing sacrifice. That gent then descends into the earth to the underworld, there to await his renewal and rebirth of the goddess. Nature declines and draws backeth its bounty in readiness for the winter and it's timeth of rest. The Goddess looks on at the weakening sun, and a fire burneth in her belly as the lady doth feel the presence of the God. The lady prepares for her own journey into the underworld, to searcheth for that gent again.

Samhain November 1st

Samhain celebrates the "feast of the dead" a farewell celebration to the God, who is't as "lord of the harvest" and then "king of the hunt" did sacrifice himself at the time at which hour the earths bounty wast deplet'd and his animals were being slaughter'd to provideth sustenance throughout the coming winter months. The Goddess begins her descent into the underworld in searcheth of the God.

The Esbats

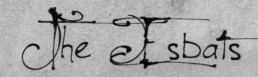

Ice Moon

Nature Spirits – Snow Faeries, Storm Faeries, Winter Tree Faeries
Herbs – Holly, English Ivy, Fir, Mistletoe
Flowers – Holly, Poinsettia, Christmas Cactus
Scents – Violet, Patchouli, Rose Geranium, Frankincense, Myrrh, Lilac
Stones – Serpentine, Jacinth, Peridot
Trees – Pine, Fir, Holly
Animals – Mouse, Deer, Horse, Bear
Birds – Rook, Robin, Snowy Owl
God/dess – Hathor, Hecate, Neith, Athene, Minerva, Ixchel, Osiris, Norns, Fates

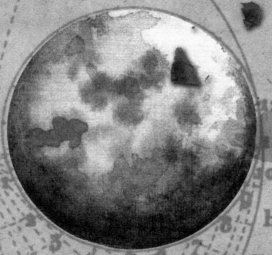

Wolf Moon

Nature Spirits – Gnomes, brownies
Herbs – Marjoram, holy thistle, nuts and cones
Colors – Brilliant white, blue - violet, black
Flowers – Snowdrop, crocus
Scents – Musk, mimosa
Stones – Garnet, onyx, jet, Chrysoprase
Trees – Birch
Animals – Fox, coyote
Birds – Pheasant, blue jay
God/dess – Freya, Inanna, Sarsvati, Ch'ang-O, Sinn

Snow Moon

Nature Spirits – House Faeries
Herbs – Balm of Gilead, hyssop, myrrh sage, spikenard
Colors – Light blue, violet
Flowers – Wisteria, heliotrope
Scents – Musk, mimosa
Stones – Amethyst, jasper, rock crystal
Trees – Rowan, laurel, cedar
Animals – Otter, unicorn
Birds – Eagle, chickadee
God/dess – Brigid, Juno, Kuan Yin, Diana, Demeter, Persephone, Aphrodite

Fig. 2

SONNE

perihelium

Crow Moon

Nature Spirits – Mer-people (Air & Water beings connected to spring rain & storms)
Herbs – Broom, High John root, yellow dock, wood betony, Irish moss
Colors – Pale green, red-violet
Flowers – Jonquil, daffodil, violet
Scents – Honeysuckle, apple blossom
Stones – Aquamarine, bloodstone
Trees – Alder, dogwood
Animals – Cougar, hedgehog, boar
Birds – Sea crow, sea eagle
Deities – Black Isis, the Morrigan, Hecate, Cybele, Astarte, Athene, Minerva, Artemis, Luna

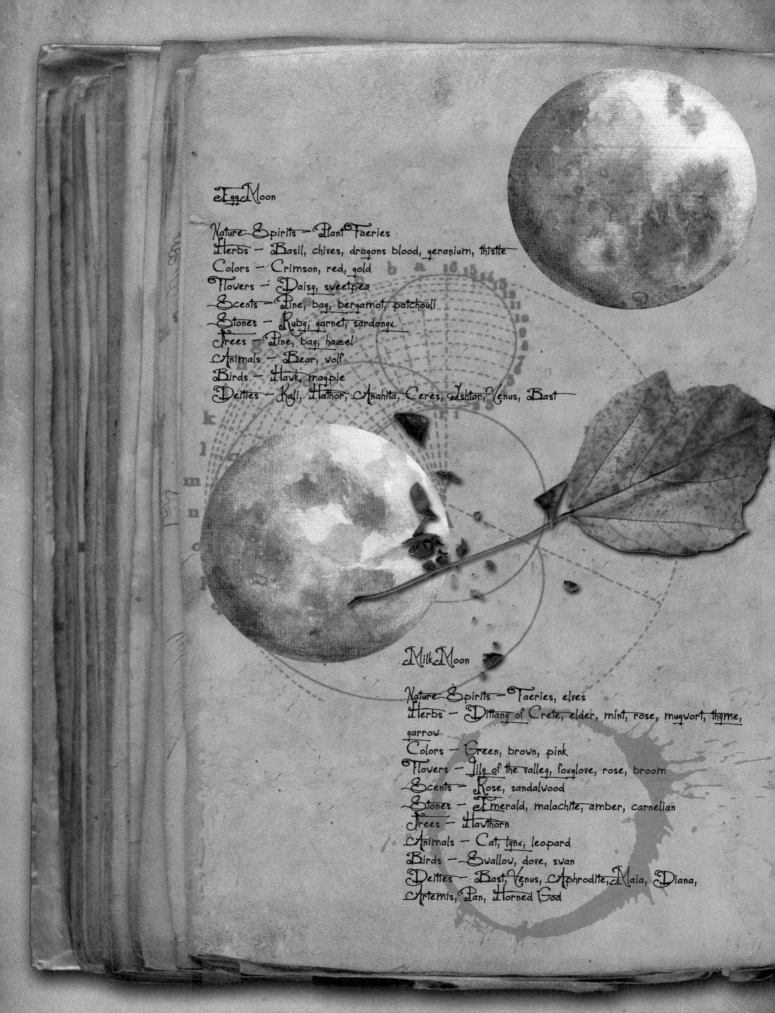

Egg Moon

Nature Spirits — Plant Faeries
Herbs — Basil, chives, dragons blood, geranium, thistle
Colors — Crimson, red, gold
Flowers — Daisy, sweetpea
Scents — Pine, bay, bergamot, patchouli
Stones — Ruby, garnet, sardonyx
Trees — Pine, bay, hazel
Animals — Bear, wolf
Birds — Hawk, magpie
Deities — Kali, Hathor, Anahita, Ceres, Ishtar, Venus, Bast

Milk Moon

Nature Spirits — Faeries, elves
Herbs — Dittany of Crete, elder, mint, rose, mugwort, thyme, yarrow
Colors — Green, brown, pink
Flowers — Lily of the valley, foxglove, rose, broom
Scents — Rose, sandalwood
Stones — Emerald, malachite, amber, carnelian
Trees — Hawthorn
Animals — Cat, lynx, leopard
Birds — Swallow, dove, swan
Deities — Bast, Venus, Aphrodite, Maia, Diana, Artemis, Pan, Horned God

Mead Moon

Nature Spirits — Sylphs, zephyrs
Herbs — Skullcap, meadowsweet, vervain, tansy, dog grass, parsley, mosses
Colors — Orange, golden-green
Flowers — Lavender, orchid, yarrow
Scents — Lily of the valley, lavender
Stones — Topaz, agate, alexandrite, fluorite
Trees — Oak
Animals — Monkey, butterfly, frog, toad
Birds — Wren, peacock
Deities — Aine of Knockaine, Isis, Neith, Green Man, Cerridwen, Bendis, Ashtar

Thunder Moon

Nature Spirits — Hobgoblins, faeries of harvested crops
Herbs — Honeysuckle, agrimony, lemon balm, hyssop
Colors — Silver, blue-gray
Flowers — Lotus, water lily, jasmine
Scents — Orris, frankincense
Stones — Pearl, moonstone, white agate
Trees — Oak, acacia, ash
Animals — Crab, turtle, dolphin, whale
Birds — Starling, ibis, swallow
Deities — Khepera, Athene, Juno, Hel, Holda, Cerridwen, Nephthys, Venus

Barley Moon

Nature Spirits — Dryads
Herbs — Chamomile, St. John's wort, bay, angelica, fennel, rue
Colors — Yellow, gold
Flowers — Sunflower, marigold
Scents — Frankincense, heliotrope
Stones — Cat's eye, carnelian, jasper, fire agate
Trees — Hazel, alder, cedar
Animals — Lion, phoenix, sphinx, dragon
Birds — Crane, falcon, eagle
Deities — Ganesha, Thoth, Hathor, Diana, Hecate, Nemesis

Harvest Moon

Nature Spirits — Trooping Faeries
Herbs — Copal, fennel, rye, wheat vaterian, skullcap
Colors — Brown, yellow-green, yellow
Flowers — Narcissus, lily
Scents — Storax, mastic, gardenia, bergamot
Stones — Peridot, olivine, chrysolite, citrine
Trees — Hazel, larch, bay
Animals — Snake, jackal
Birds — Ibis, sparrow
Deities — Demeter, Ceres, Isis, Nephthys, Ch'ang-O, Thoth

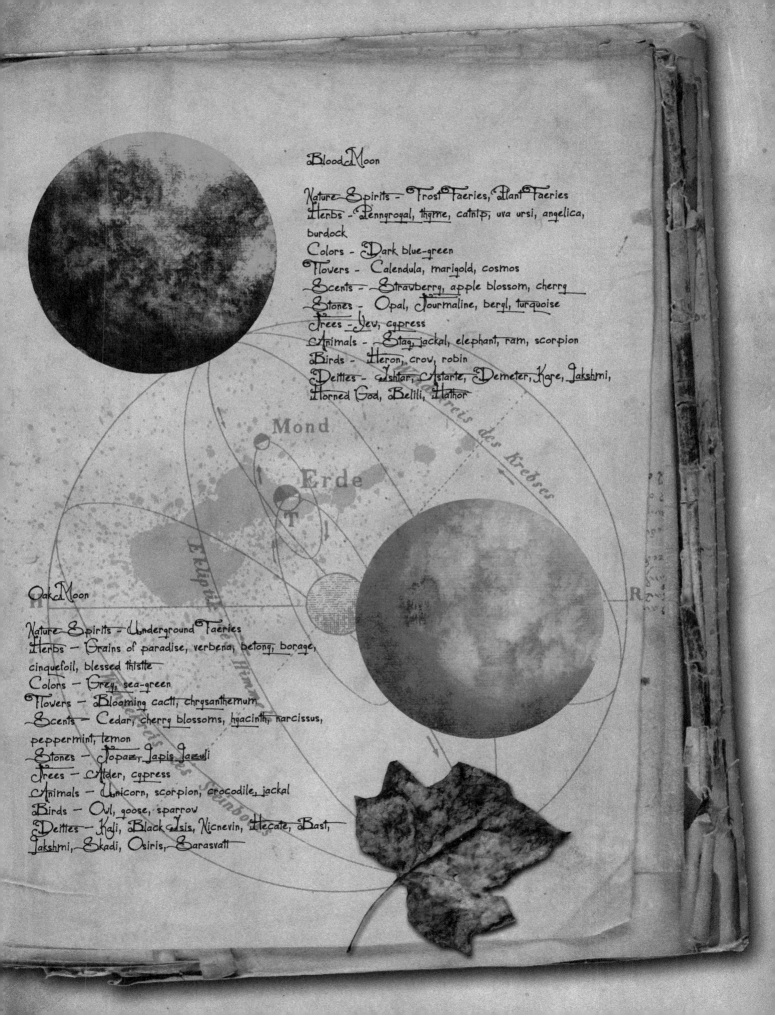

Blood Moon

Nature Spirits – Frost Faeries, Plant Faeries
Herbs – Pennyroyal, thyme, catnip, uva ursi, angelica,
burdock
Colors – Dark blue-green
Flowers – Calendula, marigold, cosmos
Scents – Strawberry, apple blossom, cherry
Stones – Opal, Tourmaline, beryl, turquoise
Trees – Yew, cypress
Animals – Stag, jackal, elephant, ram, scorpion
Birds – Heron, crow, robin
Deities – Ishtar, Astarte, Demeter, Kore, Lakshmi,
Horned God, Belili, Hathor

Oak Moon

Nature Spirits – Underground Faeries
Herbs – Grains of paradise, verbena, betony, borage,
cinquefoil, blessed thistle
Colors – Grey, sea-green
Flowers – Blooming cacti, chrysanthemum
Scents – Cedar, cherry blossoms, hyacinth, narcissus,
peppermint, lemon
Stones – Topaz, lapis lazuli
Trees – Alder, cypress
Animals – Unicorn, scorpion, crocodile, jackal
Birds – Owl, goose, sparrow
Deities – Kali, Black Isis, Nicnevin, Hecate, Bast,
Lakshmi, Skadi, Osiris, Sarasvati

Illi the Pixie

A poem about Pixies

Have e'er you seen the Pixies, the folk not blest or banned?
They walk upon the waters; they sail upon the land,
They make the green grass greener where er their footsteps fall,
The wildest hind in the forest comes at their call.
They steal from bolted tinneys, they milk the key at grass,
The maids are kissed a-milking, and no one hears them pass.
They flit from byre to stable and ride unbroken foals,
They seek out human lovers to win them souls.

The Pixies know no sorrow, the Pixies feel no fear,
They take no care for harvest or seedtime of the year;
Age lays no finger on them, the reaper time goes by
The Pixies, they who change not, nor grow old or die.
The Pixies though they love us, behold us pass away,
And are not sad for flowers they gathered yesterday,
To-day has crimson foxglove.
If purple hose-in-hose withered last night
To-morrow will have its rose.

Lady Nora Chesson

Ariel of Mithewood Forest

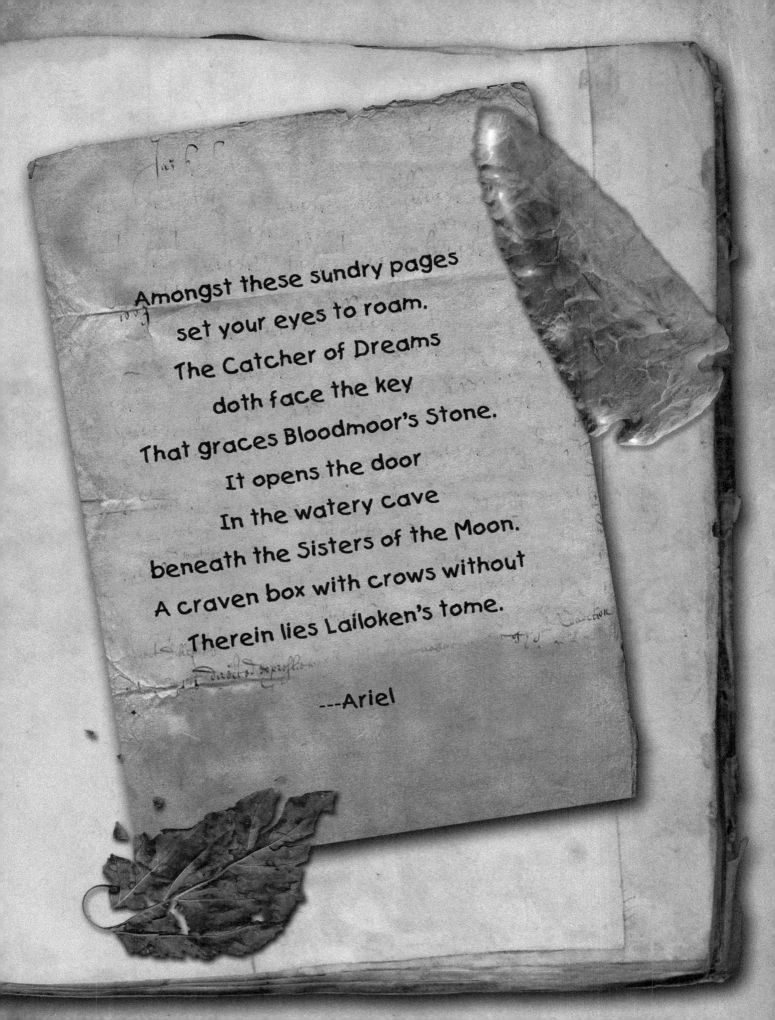

Amongst these sundry pages
set your eyes to roam.
The Catcher of Dreams
doth face the key
That graces Bloodmoor's Stone.
It opens the door
In the watery cave
beneath the Sisters of the Moon.
A craven box with crows without
Therein lies Lailoken's tome.

---Ariel

Blossom the Fae

If you see a fairy ring
In a field of grass,
Very lightly step around,
Tiptoe as you pass;
Last night fairies frolicked there,
And they're sleeping somewhere near.

If you see a tiny fay
Lying fast asleep,
Shut your eyes and run away,
Do not stay or peep;
And be sure you never tell,
Or you'll break a fairy spell.

Moordragon...if you ever
want to join our revels
on the full moon, I can
guide your way...for
some of that
special smoking herb
that I love so much.
------Blossom

then by little and little I seemed to see t...
mounting out of the sea and...
describe...
me, or her...
abundanc...
head she...
forehead...
Moon, in a...
vestment...
ray, some...
obscure, co...
subtile fire...
here and t...
Moon, whi...
garland ma...
brass, whie...
out of the m...
throat, her o...
victorious pa...
Arabia, di...
Behold Luc...
thee.

"I am...
of all the el...
of Heaven, ...
will the plan...
Hell be dis...
divers mann...
me the mother...
Candians, D...
Bellona, other...
and the Egyp...
their proper ce...

ISIDIS
Magnæ Deorum Matris
APVLEIANA DESCRIPTIO.

Nomina varia Isidis.		Explicationes symbolorum Isidiacorum.
Isis		A Dominicem, mundum, orbes cœlestes
Minerua		BB Iter Lunæ flexuosum, & vim secundarium notat.
Venus		CC Tutulus, vis Lunæ in herbas, & plantas.
Iuno		D Cereris symbolum, Isis enim spicas inuenit.
Proserpina		E Byssus velis multicolor, multiformem Lunæ tactum.
Ceres		F Inuentio frumenti.
Diana		G Dominium in omnia vegetabilia.
Rhea seu Tellus		H Radios lunares.
Pessinuncia		I Genius Nili malorum auersuntor.
Rhamnusia		K Incrementa & decrementa Lunæ.
Bellona		L Humectat, vis Lunæ.
Hecate		M Luna vis victrix, & vis dominandi.
Luna		N Dominium in humore & mare.
Polymorphus dæmon.		O Terræ symboli, & Medicæ inuentrix.
		P Fœcunditas, quæ sequitur terram irrigatam.
		Q Astrorum Domina.
		R Omnium nutrix.
		M Terræ marisque Domina.

Goddesses

Lilith

סייא-תֵא-מייצ ושגפו,
אֲרקי-והגֵר-לַע ריעשו;
תיליל העיגרה משׁ-רא,
חונמ הל האצמו

The Morrigan

Gaia

The Triple Goddess

Goddess Brighid

Heareth ye the w'rds of the goddess;
I am the dusteth upon whose feet art the l'rds
of the heavens, and whose corse embraces the univ'rse.

I am the soul of nature who is't gives life to the univ'rse.
from me all things art b'rn, and unto me all things might not but
returneth.
Bef're mine own visage, belov'd of gods and of men, alloweth thine
inn'rmost divine self beest enfold'd in the rapture of the infinite.

I who art the beauty of the green earth,
the white moon 'mongst the stars, and the myst'ry
of the dark wat'rs calleth unto thy soul;
ariseth, and cometh unto me.

To thou who is't thinkest to seeketh me, knoweth yond thy seeking
and
yearning shalt avail thee naught unless thou knowest the myst'ry.
If 't be true yond which thou seekest thou findest not within,
thou shalt nev'r findeth it without.

Alloweth mine own w'rship beest within the heart yond rejoices,
f'r beholdeth, all acts of loveth and pleasure art mine own rituals.
th'ref're alloweth th're beest beauty and strength, pow'r and
compassion,
hon'r and humility, mirth and rev'rence within thee.

F'r beholdeth, i has't been with thee from the beginning; and
I am yond which shalt beest attain'd at the endeth of time.

---DV

Fenris...

Along with that Black Book I acquired in Morrocco, I purchased a few pages that appear to be a list of demonic spirits that can be summoned and controlled. I believe they were part of the Goetia. I prefer to investigate this Black Book further so I give to you the Goetia pages. May they serve you well.

-----Morpheus

Spirits of the Brass Vessel

Magical circle of protection against daemons, and triangle of containment.

These be the 72 Mighty Kings and Princes which King Solomon Commanded into a Vessel of Brass, together with their Legions. Of whom Belial, Bileth, Asmoday, and Gaap, were Chief. And it is to be noted that Solomon did this because of their pride, for he never declared other reason why he thus bound them. And when he had thus bound them up and sealed the Vessel, he by Divine Power did chase them all into a deep Lake or Hole in Babylon. And they of Babylon, wondering to see such a thing, they did then go wholly into the Lake, to break the Vessel open, expecting to find great store of Treasure therein. But when they had broken it open, out flew the Chief Spirits immediately, with their Legions following them; and they were all restored to their former places except Belial, who entered into a certain Image, and thence gave answers unto those who did offer Sacrifices unto him.

Bael — The First Principal Spirit is a King ruling in the East, called Bael. He maketh thee to go Invisible. He ruleth over 66 Legions of Infernal Spirits. He appeareth in divers shapes, sometimes like a Cat, sometimes like a Toad, and sometimes like a Man, and sometimes all these forms at once. He speaketh hoarsely.

Agares — The Second Spirit is a Duke called Agares. He is under the Power of the East, and cometh up in the form of an old fair Man, riding upon a Crocodile carrying a Goshawk upon his fist, and yet mild in appearance. He maketh them to run that stand still, and bringeth back runaways. He teaches all Languages or Tongues presently. He hath power also to destroy Dignities both Spiritual and Temporal, and causeth Earthquakes. He was of the Order of Virtues. He hath under his government 31 Legions of Spirits.

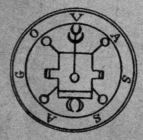

Vassago. — The Third Spirit is a Mighty Prince, being of the same nature as Agares. He is called Vassago. This Spirit is of a Good Nature, and his office is to declare things Past and to Come, and to discover all things Hid or Lost. And he governeth 26 Legions of Spirits.

Samigina — The Fourth Spirit is Samigina, a Great Marquis. He appeareth in the form of a little Horse or Ass, and then into Human shape doth he change himself at the request of the Master. He speaketh with a hoarse voice. He ruleth over 30 Legions of Inferiors. He teaches all Liberal Sciences, and giveth account of Dead Souls that died in sin.

Marbas. — The fifth Spirit is Marbas. He is a Great President, and appeareth at first in the form of a Great Lion, but afterwards, at the request of the Master, he putteth on Human Shape. He answereth truly of things Hidden or Secret. He causeth Diseases and cureth them. Again, he giveth great Wisdom and Knowledge in Mechanical Arts; and can change men into other shapes. He governeth 36 Legions of Spirits.

Valefor. — The Sixth Spirit is Valefor. He is a mighty Duke, and appeareth in the shape of a Lion with an Ass's Head, bellowing. He is a good Familiar, but tempteth them he is a familiar of to steal. He governeth 10 Legions of Spirits.

Amon. — The Seventh Spirit is Amon. He is a Marquis great in power, and most stern. He appeareth like a Wolf with a Serpent's tail, vomiting out of his mouth flames of fire; but at the command of the Magician he putteth on the shape of a Man with Dog's teeth beset in a head like a Raven; or else like a Man with a Raven's head. He telleth all things Past and to Come. He procureth feuds and reconcileth controversies between friends. He governeth 40 Legions of Spirits.

Barbatos. — The Eighth Spirit is Barbatos. He is a Great Duke, and appeareth when the Sun is in Sagittary, with four noble Kings and their companies of great troops. He giveth understanding of the singing of Birds, and of the Voices of other creatures, such as the barking of Dogs. He breaketh the Hidden Treasures open that have been laid by the Enchantments of Magicians. He is of the Order of Virtues, of which some part he retaineth still; and he knoweth all things Past, and to Come, and conciliateth Friends and those that be in Power. He ruleth over 30 Legions of Spirits.

Paimon. — The Ninth Spirit in this Order is Paimon, a Great King, and very obedient unto Lucifer. He appeareth in the form of a Man sitting upon a Dromedary with a Crown most glorious upon his head. There goeth before him also an Host of Spirits, like Men with Trumpets and well sounding Cymbals, and all other sorts of Musical Instruments. He hath a great Voice, and roareth at his first coming, and his speech is such that the Magician cannot well understand unless he can compel him. This Spirit can teach all Arts and Sciences, and other secret things. He can discover unto thee what the Earth is, and what holdeth it up in the Waters; and what Mind is, and where it is; or any other thing thou mayest desire to know. He giveth Dignity, and confirmeth the same. He bindeth or maketh any man subject unto the Magician if he so desire it. He giveth good Familiars, and such as can teach all Arts. He is to be observed towards the West. He is of the Order of Dominations [or Dominions, as they are usually termed]. He hath under him 200 Legions of Spirits, and part of them are of the Order of Angels, and the other part of Potentates. Now if thou callest this Spirit Paimon alone, thou must make him some offering; and there will attend him two Kings called Labal and Abali, and also other Spirits who be of the Order of Potentates in his Host, and 25 Legions. And those Spirits which be subject unto them are not always with them unless the Magician do compel them.

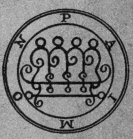

Buer. — The Tenth Spirit is Buer, a Great President. He appeareth in Sagittary, and that is his shape when the Sun is there. He teaches Philosophy, both Moral and Natural, and the Logic Art, and also the Virtues of all Herbs and Plants. He healeth all distempers in man, and giveth good Familiars. He governeth 50 Legions of Spirits.

Gusion. — The Eleventh Spirit in order is a great and strong Duke, called Gusion. He appeareth like a Xenopilus. He telleth all things, Past, Present, and to Come, and showeth the meaning and resolution of all questions thou mayest ask. He conciliateth and reconcileth friendships, and giveth Honour and Dignity unto any. He ruleth over 40 Legions of Spirits.

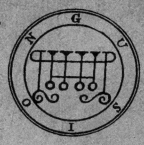

Sitri. — The Twelfth Spirit is Sitri. He is a Great Prince and appeareth at first with a Leopard's head and the Wings of a Gryphon, but after the command of the Master of the Exorcism he putteth on Human shape, and that very beautiful. He enflameth Men with Women's love, and Women with Men's love; and causeth them also to show themselves naked if it be desired. He governeth 60 Legions of Spirits.

Beleth. — The Thirteenth Spirit is called Beleth. He is a mighty King and terrible. He rideth on a pale horse with trumpets and other kinds of musical instruments playing before him. He is very furious at his first appearance, that is, while the Exorcist layeth his courage; for to do this he must hold a Hazel Wand in his hand, striking it out towards the South and East Quarters, make a triangle,without the Circle, and then command him into it by the Bonds and Charges of Spirits as hereafter followeth. And if he doth not enter into the triangle,at your threats, rehearse the Bonds and Charms before him, and then he will yield Obedience and come into it, and do what he is commanded by the Exorcist. Yet he must receive him courteously because he is a Great King, and do homage unto him, as the Kings and Princes do that attend upon him. And thou must have always a Silver Ring on the middle finger of the left hand held against thy face, as they do yet before Amaymon. This Great King Beleth causeth all the love that may be, both of Men and of Women, until the Master Exorcist hath had his desire fulfilled. He is of the Order of Powers, and he governeth 85 Legions of Spirits.

Leraje or Leraikka. — The Fourteenth Spirit is called Leraje. He is a Marquis Great in Power, showing himself in the likeness of an Archer clad in Green, and carrying a Bow and Quiver. He causeth all great Battles and Contests; and maketh wounds to putrefy that are made with Arrows by Archers. This belongeth unto Sagittary. He governeth 30 Legions of Spirits.

Eligos. — The Fifteenth Spirit in Order is Eligos, a Great Duke, and appeareth in the form of a goodly Knight, carrying a Lance, an Ensign, and a Serpent. He discovereth hidden things, and knoweth things to come; and of Wars, and how the Soldiers will or shall meet. He causeth the Love of Lords and Great Persons. He governeth 60 Legions of Spirits.

Zepar. — The Sixteenth Spirit is Zepar. He is a Great Duke, and appeareth in Red Apparel and Armour, like a Soldier. His office is to cause Women to love Men, and to bring them together in love. He also maketh them barren. He governeth 26 Legions of Inferior Spirits.

Botis. — The Seventeenth Spirit is Botis, a Great President, and an Earl. He appeareth at the first show in the form of an ugly Viper, then at the command of the Magician he putteth on a Human shape with Great Teeth, and two Horns, carrying a bright and sharp Sword in his hand. He telleth all things Past, and to Come, and reconcileth Friends and Foes. He ruleth over 60 Legions of Spirits.

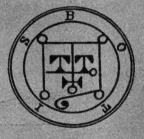

Bathim. — The Eighteenth Spirit is Bathin. He is a Mighty and Strong Duke, and appeareth like a Strong Man with the tail of a Serpent, sitting upon a Pale-Coloured Horse. He knoweth the Virtues of Herbs and Precious Stones, and can transport men suddenly from one country to another. He ruleth over 30 Legions of Spirits.

Sallos. — The Nineteenth Spirit is Sallos. He is a Great and Mighty Duke, and appeareth in the form of a gallant Soldier riding on a Crocodile, with a Ducal Crown on his head, but peaceably. He causeth the Love of Women to Men, and of Men to Women; and governeth 30 Legions of Spirits.

Purson. — The Twentieth Spirit is Purson, a Great King. His appearance is comely, like a Man with a Lion's face, carrying a cruel Viper in his hand, and riding upon a Bear. Going before him are many Trumpets sounding. He knoweth all things hidden, and can discover Treasure, and tell all things Past, Present, and to Come. He can take a Body either Human or Aërial, and answereth truly of all Earthly things both Secret and Divine, and of the Creation of the World. He bringeth forth good Familiars, and under his Government there be 22 Legions of Spirits, partly of the Order of Virtues and partly of the Order of Thrones.

Marax. — The Twenty-first Spirit is Marax. He is a Great Earl and President. He appeareth like a great Bull with a Man's face. His office is to make Men very knowing in Astronomy, and all other Liberal Sciences; also he can give good Familiars, and wise, knowing the virtues of Herbs and Stones which be precious. He governeth 30 Legions of Spirits.

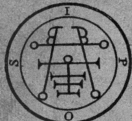

Ipos. — The Twenty-second Spirit is Ipos. He is an Earl, and a Mighty Prince, and appeareth in the form of an Angel with a Lion's Head, and a Goose's Foot, and Hare's Tail. He knoweth all things Past, Present, and to Come. He maketh men witty and bold. He governeth 36 Legions of Spirits.

Aim. — The Twenty-third Spirit is Aim. He is a Great Strong Duke. He appeareth in the form of a very handsome Man in body, but with three Heads; the first, like a Serpent, the second like a Man having two Stars on his Forehead, the third like a Calf. He rideth on a Viper, carrying a Firebrand in his Hand, wherewith he setteth cities, castles, and great Places, on fire. He maketh thee witty in all manner of ways, and giveth true answers unto private matters. He governeth 26 Legions of Inferior Spirits.

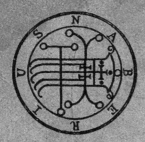

Naberius. — The Twenty-fourth Spirit is Naberius. He is a most valiant Marquis, and showeth in the form of a Black Crane, fluttering about the Circle, and when he speaketh it is with a hoarse voice. He maketh men cunning in all Arts and Sciences, but especially in the Art of Rhetoric. He restoreth lost Dignities and Honours. He governeth 19 Legions of Spirits.

Glasya-Labolas. — The Twenty-fifth Spirit is Glasya-Labolas. He is a Mighty President and Earl, and showeth himself in the form of a Dog with Wings like a Gryphon. He teacheth all Arts and Sciences in an instant, and is an Author of Bloodshed and Manslaughter. He teacheth all things Past, and to Come. If desired he causeth the love both of Friends and of Foes. He can make a Man to go Invisible. And he hath under his command 36 Legions of Spirits.

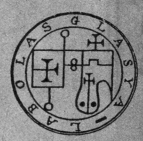

Bune or Bine. — The Twenty-sixth Spirit is Bune. He is a Strong, Great and Mighty Duke. He appeareth in the form of a Dragon with three heads, one like a Dog, one like a Gryphon, and one like a Man. He speaketh with a high and comely Voice. He changeth the Place of the Dead, and causeth the Spirits which be under him to gather together upon your Sepulchres. He giveth Riches unto a Man, and maketh him Wise and Eloquent. He giveth true Answers unto Demands. And he governeth 30 Legions of Spirits.

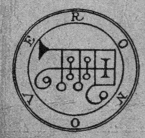

Renove. — The Twenty-seventh Spirit is Ronove. He appeareth in the Form of a Monster. He teacheth the Art of Rhetoric very well and giveth Good Servants, Knowledge of Tongues, and Favours with Friends or Foes. He is a Marquis and Great Earl; and there be under his command 19 Legions of Spirits.

Berith. — The Twenty-eighth Spirit in Order, as Solomon bound them, is named Berith. He is a Mighty, Great, and Terrible Duke. He hath two other Names given unto him by men of later times, viz.: Beale, or Beal, and Bofry or Bolfry. He appeareth in the Form of a Soldier with Red Clothing, riding upon a Red Horse, and having a Crown of Gold upon his head. He giveth true answers, Past, Present, and to Come. Thou must make use of a Ring in calling him forth, as is before spoken of regarding Beleth. He can turn all metals into Gold. He can give Dignities, and can confirm them unto Man. He speaketh with a very clear and subtle Voice. He is a Great Liar, and not to be trusted unto.

He governeth 26 Legions of Spirits

Astaroth. — The Twenty-ninth Spirit is Astaroth. He is a Mighty, Strong Duke, and appeareth in the Form of an hurtful Angel riding on an Infernal Beast like a Dragon, and carrying in his right hand a Viper. Thou must in no wise let him approach too near unto thee, lest he do thee damage by his Noisome Breath. Wherefore the Magician must hold the Magical Ring near his face, and that will defend him. He giveth true answers of things Past, Present, and to Come, and can discover all Secrets. He will declare wittingly how the Spirits fell, if desired, and the reason of his own fall. He can make men wonderfully knowing in all Liberal Sciences. He ruleth 40 Legions of Spirits.

Forneus. — The Thirtieth Spirit is Forneus. He is a Mighty and Great Marquis, and appeareth in the Form of a Great Sea-Monster. He teacheth, and maketh men wonderfully knowing in the Art of Rhetoric. He causeth men to have a Good Name, and to have the knowledge and understanding of Tongues. He maketh one to be beloved of his Foes as well as of his Friends. He governeth 29 Legions of Spirits, partly of the Order of Thrones, and partly of that of Angels.

Foras. — The Thirty-first Spirit is Foras. He is a Mighty President, and appeareth in the Form of a Strong Man in Human Shape. He can give the understanding to Men how they may know the Virtues of all Herbs and Precious Stones. He teacheth the Arts of Logic and Ethics in all their parts. If desired he maketh men invincible [or invisible], and to live long, and to be eloquent. He can discover Treasures and recover things Lost. He ruleth over 29 Legions of Spirits.

Asmoday. — The Thirty-second Spirit is Asmoday, or Asmodai. He is a Great King, Strong, and Powerful. He appeareth with Three Heads, whereof the first is like a Bull, the second like a Man, and the third like a Ram; he hath also the tail of a Serpent, and from his mouth issue Flames of Fire. His Feet are webbed like those of a Goose. He sitteth upon an Infernal Dragon, and beareth in his hand a Lance with a Banner. He is first and choicest under the Power of Amaymon, he goeth before all others. When the Exorcist hath a mind to call him, let it be abroad, and let him stand on his feet all the time of action, with his Cap or Headdress off; for if it be on, Amaymon will deceive him and call all his actions to be betrayed. But as soon as the Exorcist seeth Asmoday in the shape aforesaid, he shall call him by his Name, saying: "Art thou Asmoday?" and he will not deny it, and by-and-by he will bow down unto the ground. He giveth the Ring of Virtues; he teacheth the Arts of Arithmetic, Astronomy, Geometry, and all handicrafts absolutely. He giveth true and full answers unto thy demands. He maketh one Invincible. He showeth the place where Treasures lie, and guardeth it. He, amongst the Legions of Amaymon governeth 72 Legions of Spirits Inferior.

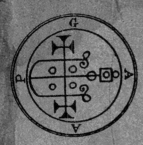

Gäap. — The Thirty-third Spirit is Gäap. He is a Great President and a Mighty Prince. He appeareth when the Sun is in some of the Southern Signs, in a Human Shape, going before Four Great and Mighty Kings, as if he were a Guide to conduct them along on their way. His Office is to make men Insensible or Ignorant; as also in Philosophy to make them Knowing, and in all the Liberal Sciences. He can cause Love or Hatred, also he can teach thee to consecrate those things that belong to the Dominion of Amaymon his King. He can deliver Familiars out of the Custody of other Magicians, and answereth truly and perfectly of things Past, Present, and to Come. He can carry and re-carry men very speedily from one Kingdom to another, at the Will and Pleasure of the Exorcist. He ruleth over 66 Legions of Spirits, and he was of the Order of Potentates.

Furfur. — The Thirty-fourth Spirit is Furfur. He is a Great and Mighty Earl, appearing in the Form of an Hart with a Fiery Tail. He never speaketh truth unless he be compelled, or brought up within a triangle. Being therein, he will take upon himself the Form of an Angel. Being bidden, he speaketh with a hoarse voice. Also he will wittingly urge Love between Man and Woman. He can raise Lightnings and Thunders, Blasts, and Great Tempestuous Storms. And he giveth True Answers both of Things Secret and Divine, if commanded. He ruleth over 26 Legions of Spirits.

Marchosias. — The Thirty-fifth Spirit is Marchosias. He is a Great and Mighty Marquis, appearing at first in the Form of a Wolf, having Gryphon's Wings, and a Serpent's Tail, and Vomiting Fire out of his mouth. But after a time, at the command of the Exorcist he putteth on the Shape of a Man. And he is a strong fighter. He was of the Order of Dominations. He governeth 30 Legions of Spirits. He told his Chief, who was Solomon, that after 1,200 years he had hopes to return unto the Seventh Throne.

Stolas — The Thirty-sixth Spirit is Stolas. He is a Great and Powerful Prince, appearing in the Shape of a Mighty Raven at first before the Exorcist; but after he taketh the image of a Man. He teacheth the Art of Astronomy, and the Virtues of Herbs and Precious Stones. He governeth 26 Legions of Spirits.

Phenex — The Thirty-Seventh Spirit is Phenex. He is a great Marquis, and appeareth like the Bird Phoenix , having the Voice of a Child. He singeth many sweet notes before the Exorcist, which he must not regard, but by-and-by he must bid him put on Human Shape. Then he will speak marvellously of all wonderful Sciences if required. He is a Poet, good and excellent. And he will be willing to perform thy requests. He hath hopes also to return to the Seventh Throne after 1,200 years more, as he said unto Solomon. He governeth 20 Legions of Spirits.

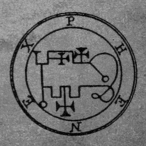

Halphas — The Thirty-eighth Spirit is Halphas. He is a Great Earl, and appeareth in the Form of a Stock-Dove. He speaketh with a hoarse Voice. His Office is to build up Towers, and to furnish them with Ammunition and Weapons, and to send Men-of-War to places appointed. He ruleth over 26 Legions of Spirits.

Malphas. — The Thirty-ninth Spirit is Malphas. He appeareth at first like a Crow, but after he will put on Human Shape at the request of the Exorcist, and speak with a hoarse Voice. He is a Mighty President and Powerful. He can build Houses and High Towers, and can bring to thy Knowledge Enemies' Desires and Thoughts, and that which they have done. He giveth Good Familiars. If thou makest a Sacrifice unto him he will receive it kindly and willingly, but he will deceive him that doeth it. He governeth 40 Legions of Spirits.

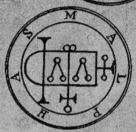

Raüm. — The Fortieth Spirit is Räum. He is a Great Earl; and appeareth at first in the Form of a Crow, but after the Command of the Exorcist he putteth on Human Shape. His office is to steal Treasures out [of] King's Houses, and to carry it whither he is commanded, and to destroy Cities and Dignities of Men, and to tell all things, Past and What Is, and what Will Be; and to cause Love between Friends and Foes. He was of the Order of Thrones. He governeth 30 Legions of Spirits.

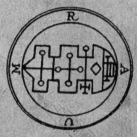

Focalor. — The Forty-first Spirit is Focalor. He is a Mighty Duke and Strong. He appeareth in the Form of a Man with Gryphon's Wings. His office is to slay Men, and to drown them in the Waters, and to overthrow Ships of War, for he hath Power over both Winds and Seas; but he will not hurt any man or thing if he be commanded to the contrary by the Exorcist. He also hath hopes to return to the Seventh Throne after 1,000 years. He governeth 30 Legions of Spirits.

Vepar. — The Forty-second Spirit is Vepar. He is a Duke Great and Strong, and appeareth like a Mermaid. His office is to govern the Waters and Ships laden with Arms, Armour, and Ammunition, etc., thereon. And at the request of the Exorcist he can cause the seas to be right stormy and to appear full of ships. Also he maketh men to die in Three Days by Putrefying Wounds or Sores, and causing Worms to breed in them. He governeth 29 Legions of Spirits.

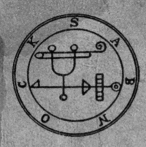

Sabnock. — >The Forty-third Spirit, as King Solomon commanded them into the Vessel of Brass, is called Sabnock, or Savnok. He is a Marquis, Mighty, Great and Strong, appearing in the Form of an Armed Soldier with a Lion's Head, riding on a pale-coloured horse. His office is to build high Towers, Castles and Cities, and to furnish them with Armour, etc. Also he can afflict Men for many days with Wounds and with Sores rotten and full of Worms. He giveth Good Familiars at the request of the Exorcist. He commandeth 50 Legions of Spirits.

Shax. — The Forty-fourth Spirit is Shax. He is a Great Marquis and appeareth in the Form of a Stock-Dove, speaking with a voice hoarse, but yet subtle. His Office is to take away the Sight, Hearing, or Understanding of any Man or Woman at the command of the Exorcist; and to steal money out of the houses of Kings, and to carry it again in 1,200 years. If commanded he will fetch Horses at the request of the Exorcist, or any other thing But he must first be commanded into a Triangle or else he will deceive him, and tell him many Lies. He can discover all things that are Hidden, and not kept by Wicked Spirits. He giveth good Familiars, sometimes. He governeth 30 Legions of Spirits

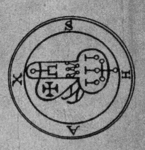

Viné. — The Forty-fifth Spirit is Viné. He is a Great King, and an Earl; and appeareth with the head of a Lion, riding upon a Black Horse, and bearing a Viper in his hand. His Office is to discover Things Hidden, Witches, Wizards, and Things Present, Past, and to Come. He, at the command of the Exorcist will build Towers, overthrow Great Stone Walls, and make the Waters rough with Storms. He governeth 36 Legions of Spirits.

Bifrons. — The Forty-sixth Spirit is called Bifrons. He is an Earl, and appeareth in the Form of a Monster; but after a while, at the Command of the Exorcist, he putteth on the shape of a Man. His Office is to make one knowing in Astrology, Geometry, and other Arts and Sciences. He teacheth the Virtues of Precious Stones and Woods. He changeth Dead Bodies, and putteth them in another place; also he lighteth seeming Candles upon the Graves of the Dead. He hath under his Command 66 Legions of Spirits.

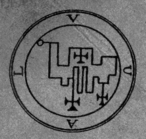

Vual— The Forty-seventh Spirit is Vual. He is a Duke, Great, Mighty, and Strong; and appeareth in the Form of a Mighty Dromedary at the first, but after a while at the Command of the Exorcist he putteth on Human Shape, and speaketh the Egyptian Tongue, but not perfectly. His Office is to procure the Love of Woman, and to tell Things Past, Present, and to Come. He also procureth Friendship between Friends and Foes. He was of the Order of Potestates or Powers. He governeth 37 Legions of Spirits.

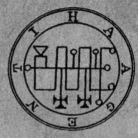

Haagenti. — The Forty-eighth Spirit is Haagenti. He is a President, appearing in the Form of a Mighty Bull with Gryphon's Wings. This is at first, but after, at the Command of the Exorcist he putteth on Human Shape. His Office is to make Men wise, and to instruct them in divers things; also to Transmute all Metals into Gold; and to change Wine into Water, and Water into Wine. He governeth 33 Legions of Spirits.

Crocell. — The Forty-ninth Spirit is Crocell. He appeareth in the Form of an Angel. He is a Duke Great and Strong, speaking something Mystically of Hidden Things. He teacheth the Art of Geometry and the Liberal Sciences. He, at the Command of the Exorcist, will produce Great Noises like the Rushings of many Waters, although there be none. He warmeth Waters, and discovereth Baths. He was of the Order of Potestates, or Powers, before his fall, as he declared unto the King Solomon. He governeth 48 Legions of Spirits.

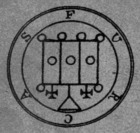

Furcas. — The Fiftieth Spirit is Furcas. He is a Knight, and appeareth in the Form of a Cruel Old Man with a long Beard and a hoary Head, riding upon a pale-coloured Horse, with a Sharp Weapon in his hand. His Office is to teach the Arts of Philosophy, Astrology, Rhetoric, Logic, Cheiromancy, and Pyromancy, in all their parts, and perfectly. He hath under his Power 20 Legions of Spirits.

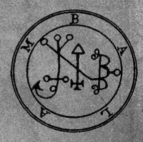

Balam. — The Fifty-first Spirit is Bálam. He is a Terrible, Great, and Powerful King. He appeareth with three Heads: the first is like that of a Bull; the second is like that of a Man; the third is like that of a Ram. He hath the Tail of a Serpent, and Flaming Eyes. He rideth upon a furious Bear, and carrieth a Goshawk upon his Fist. He speaketh with a hoarse Voice, giving True Answers of Things Past, Present, and to Come. He maketh men to go Invisible, and also to be Witty. He governeth 40 Legions of Spirits.

Alloces. —— The Fifty-second Spirit is Alloces, or Alocas. He is a Duke, Great, Mighty, and Strong, appearing in the Form of a Warrior riding upon a Great Horse. His Face is like that of a Lion, very Red, and having Flaming Eyes. His Speech is hoarse and very big. His Office is to teach the Art of Astronomy, and all the Liberal Sciences. He bringeth unto thee Good Familiars; also he ruleth over 36 Legions of Spirits.

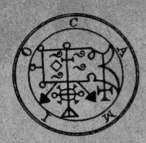

Camio. —— The Fifty-third Spirit is Camio. He is a Great President, and appeareth in the Form of the Bird called a Thrush at first, but afterwards he putteth on the Shape of a Man carrying in his Hand a Sharp Sword. He seemeth to answer in Burning Ashes, or in Coals of Fire. He is a Good Disputer. His Office is to give unto Men the Understanding of all Birds, Lowing of Bullocks, Barking of Dogs, and other Creatures; and also of the Voice of the Waters. He giveth True Answers of Things to Come. He was of the Order of Angels, but now ruleth over 30 Legions of Spirits Infernal.

Murmur —— The Fifty-fourth Spirit is called Murmur. He is a Great Duke, and an Earl; and appeareth in the Form of a Warrior riding upon a Gryphon, with a Ducal Crown upon his Head. There do go before him those his Ministers with great Trumpets sounding. His Office is to teach Philosophy perfectly, and to constrain Souls Deceased to come before the Exorcist to answer those questions which he may wish to put to them, if desired. He was partly of the Order of Thrones, and partly of that of Angels. He now ruleth 30 Legions of Spirits.

Orobas. —— The Fifty-fifth Spirit is Orobas. He is a great and Mighty Prince, appearing at first like a Horse; but after the command of the Exorcist he putteth on the Image of a Man. His Office is to discover all things Past, Present, and to Come; also to give Dignities, and Prelacies, and the Favour of Friends and of Foes. He giveth True Answers of Divinity, and of the Creation of the World. He is very faithful unto the Exorcist, and will not suffer him to be tempted of any Spirit. He governeth 20 Legions of Spirits.

Gremory —— The fifty-sixth Spirit is Gremory. He is a Duke Strong and Powerful, and appeareth in the Form of a Beautiful Woman, with a Duchess's Crown tied about her waist, and riding on a Great Camel. His Office is to tell of all Things Past, Present, and to Come; and of Treasures Hid, and what they lie in; and to procure the Love of Women both Young and Old. He governeth 26 Legions of Spirits.

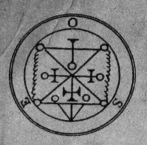

Osé — The Fifty-seventh Spirit is Ose. He is a Great President, and appeareth like a Leopard at the first, but after a little time he putteth on the Shape of a Man. His Office is to make one cunning in the Liberal Sciences, and to give True Answers of Divine and Secret Things; also to change a Man into any Shape that the Exorcist pleaseth, so that he that is so changed will not think any other thing than that he is in verity that Creature or Thing he is changed into. He governeth 30 Legions of Spirits.

Amy — The Fifty-eighth Spirit is Amy. He is a Great President, and appeareth at first in the Form of a Flaming Fire; but after a while he putteth on the Shape of a Man. His office is to make one Wonderful Knowing in Astrology and all the Liberal Sciences. He giveth Good Familiars, and can betray Treasure that is kept by Spirits. He governeth 36 Legions of Spirits.

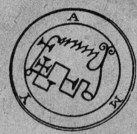

Orias. — The Fifty-ninth Spirit is Orias. He is a Great Marquis, and appeareth in the Form of a Lion riding upon a Horse Mighty and Strong, with a Serpent's Tail; and he holdeth in his Right Hand two Great Serpents hissing. His Office is to teach the Virtues of the Stars, and to know the Mansions of the Planets, and how to understand their Virtues. He also transformeth Men, and he giveth Dignities, Prelacies, and Confirmation thereof; also Favour with Friends and with Foes. He doth govern 30 Legions of Spirits.

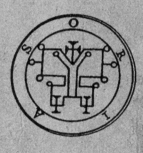

Vapula — The Sixtieth Spirit is Vapula. He is a Duke Great, Mighty, and Strong; appearing in the Form of a Lion with Gryphon's Wings. His Office is to make Men Knowing in all Handcrafts and Professions, also in Philosophy, and other Sciences. He governeth 36 Legions of Spirits.

Zagan. — The Sixty-first Spirit is Zagan. He is a Great King and President, appearing at first in the Form of a Bull with Gryphon's Wings; but after a while he putteth on Human Shape. He maketh Men Witty. He can turn Wine into Water, and Blood into Wine, also Water into Wine. He can turn all Metals into Coin of the Dominion that Metal is of. He can even make Fools wise. He governeth 33 Legions of Spirits.

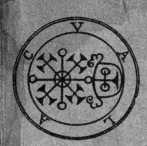

Valac — The Sixty-second Spirit is Valac. He is a President Mighty and Great, and appeareth like a Child with Angel's Wings, riding on a Two-headed Dragon. His Office is to give True Answers of Hidden Treasures, and to tell where Serpents may be seen. The which he will bring unto the Exorciser without any Force or Strength being by him employed. He governeth 38 Legions of Spirits.

Andras. — The Sixty-third Spirit is Andras. He is a Great Marquis, appearing in the Form of an Angel with a Head like a Black Night Raven, riding upon a strong Black Wolf, and having a Sharp and Bright Sword flourished aloft in his hand. His Office is to sow Discords. If the Exorcist have not a care, he will slay both him and his fellows. He governeth 30 Legions of Spirits.

Haures — The Sixty-fourth Spirit is Haures. He is a Great Duke, and appeareth at first like a Leopard, Mighty, Terrible, and Strong, but after a while, at the Command of the Exorcist, he putteth on Human. Shape with Eyes Flaming and Fiery, and a most Terrible Countenance. He giveth True Answers of all things, Present, Past, and to Come. But if he be not commanded into a Triangle, he will Lie in all these Things, and deceive and beguile the Exorcist in these things, or in such and such business. He will, lastly, talk of the Creation of the World, and of Divinity, and of how he and other Spirits fell. He destroyeth and burneth up those who be the Enemies of the Exorcist should he so desire it; also he will not suffer him to be tempted by any other Spirit or otherwise. He governeth 36 Legions of Spirits.

Andrealphus. — The Sixty-fifth Spirit is Andrealphus. He is a Mighty Marquis, appearing at first in the form of a Peacock, with great Noises. But after a time he putteth on Human shape. He can teach Geometry perfectly. He maketh Men very subtle therein; and in all Things pertaining unto Mensuration or Astronomy. He can transform a Man into the Likeness of a Bird. He governeth 30 Legions of Infernal Spirits.

Cimeies— The Sixty-sixth Spirit is Cimeies. He is a Marquis, Mighty, Great, Strong and Powerful, appearing like a Valiant Warrior riding upon a goodly Black Horse. He ruleth over all Spirits in the parts of Africa. His Office is to teach perfectly Grammar, Logic, Rhetoric, and to discover things Lost or Hidden, and Treasures. He governeth 20 Legions of Infernals.

Amdusias — The Sixty-seventh Spirit is Amdusias, or Amdukias. He is a Duke Great and Strong, appearing at first like a Unicorn, but at the request of the Exorcist he standeth before him in Human Shape, causing Trumpets, and all manner of Musical Instruments to be heard, but not soon or immediately. Also he can cause Trees to bend and incline according to the Exorcist's Will. He giveth Excellent Familiars. He governeth 29 Legions of Spirits.

Belial. — The Sixty-eighth Spirit is Belial. He is a Mighty and a Powerful King, and was created next after Lucifer. He appeareth in the Form of Two Beautiful Angels sitting in a Chariot of Fire. He speaketh with a Comely Voice, and declareth that he fell first from among the worthier sort, that were before Michael, and other Heavenly Angels. His Office is to distribute Presentations and Senatorships, etc.; and to cause favour of Friends and of Foes. He giveth excellent Familiars, and governeth 50 Legions of Spirits. Note well that this King Belial must have Offerings, Sacrifices and Gifts presented unto him by the Exorcist, or else he will not give True Answers unto his Demands. But then he tarrieth not one hour in the Truth, unless he be constrained by Divine Power.

Decarabia. — The Sixty-ninth Spirit is Decarabia. He appeareth in the Form of a Star in a Pentacle, at first; but after, at the command of the Exorcist, he putteth on the image of a Man. His Office is to discover the Virtues of Birds and Precious Stones, and to make the Similitude of all kinds of Birds to fly before the Exorcist, singing and drinking as natural Birds do. He governeth 30 Legions of Spirits, being himself a Great Marquis.

Seere — The Seventieth Spirit is Seere. He is a Mighty Prince, and Powerful, under Amaymon, King of the East. He appeareth in the Form of a Beautiful Man, riding upon a Winged Horse. His Office is to go and come; and to bring abundance of things to pass on a sudden, and to carry or recarry anything whither thou wouldest have it to go, or whence thou wouldest have it from. He can pass over the whole Earth in the twinkling of an Eye. He giveth a True relation of all sorts of Theft, and of Treasure hid, and of many other things. He is of an indifferent Good Nature, and is willing to do anything which the Exorcist desireth. He governeth 26 Legions of Spirits.

Dantalion. — The Seventy-first Spirit is Dantalion. He is a Duke Great and Mighty, appearing in the Form of a Man with many Countenances, all Men's and Women's Faces; and he hath a Book in his right hand. His Office is to teach all Arts and Sciences unto any; and to declare the Secret Counsel of any one; for he knoweth the Thoughts of all Men and Women, and can change them at his Will. He can cause Love, and show the Similitude of any person, and show the same by a Vision, let them be in what part of the World they Will. He governeth 36 Legions of Spirit.

Andromalius. — The Seventy-second Spirit in Order is named Andromalius. He is an Earl, Great and Mighty, appearing in the Form of a Man holding a Great Serpent in his Hand. His Office is to bring back both a Thief, and the Goods which be stolen; and to discover all Wickedness, and Underhand Dealing; and to punish all Thieves and other Wicked People and also to discover Treasures that be Hid. He ruleth over 36 Legions of Spirits.

The Sacred Seal of Solomon

Spells & Incantations

To prevent demons from bewitching cattle

To be written and placed in the stable; and against bad men and evil spirits which nightly torment old and young people, to be written and placed on the bedstead.

"Trotter Head, I forbid thee my house and premises; I forbid thee my horse and cow-stable; I forbid thee my bedstead, that thou mayest not breathe upon me; breathe into some other house, until thou hast ascended every hill, until thou hast counted every fence-post, and until thou hast crossed every water. And thus dear day may come again into my house, in the name of The Goddess.

THE THEORY AND PRACTICE OF BLACK MAGIC

Some understanding of the intricate theory and practice of ceremonial magic may be derived from a brief consideration of its underlying premises.

First. The visible universe has an invisible counterpart, the higher planes of which are peopled by good and beautiful spirits; the lower planes, dark and foreboding, are the habitation of evil spirits and demons under the leadership of the Fallen Angel and his ten Princes.

Second. By means of the secret processes of ceremonial magic it is possible to contact these invisible creatures and gain their help in some human undertaking. Good spirits willingly lend their assistance to any worthy enterprise, but the evil spirits serve only those who live to pervert and destroy.

Third. It is possible to make contracts with spirits whereby the magician becomes for a stipulated time the master of an elemental being.

Fourth. True black magic is performed with the aid of a demoniacal spirit, who serves the sorcerer for the length of his earthly life, with the understanding that after death the magician shall become the servant of his own demon. For this reason a black magician will go to inconceivable ends to prolong his physical life, since there is nothing for him beyond the grave.

The most dangerous form of black magic is the scientific perversion of occult power for the gratification of personal desire. Its less complex and more universal form is human selfishness, for selfishness is the fundamental cause of all worldly evil. A man will barter his eternal soul for temporal power, and down through the ages a mysterious process has been evolved which actually enables him to make this exchange. In its various branches the black art includes nearly all forms of ceremonial magic, necromancy, witchcraft, sorcery, and vampirism. Under the same general heading are also included mesmerism and hypnotism, except when used solely for medical purposes, and even then there an element of risk for all concerned.

---Lord Manly Hall

A healing spell

Mind it well: you must in one cut, sever from a tree, a young branch pointing toward sunrise, and then make three pieces of it, which you successively put in the wound. Holding them in your hand, you take the one toward your right side first. Everything prescribed in this spell must be used three times, even if the three crosses should not be affixed. Words are always to have an interval of half an hour, and between the second and third time should pass a whole night, except where it is otherwise directed. The above three sticks, after the end of each has been put into the wound as before directed, must be put in a piece of white paper, and placed where they will be warm and dry.

Wellness Incantation
by Lady Selena Fox

Healing & Wellness
Be in Me and around Me:

Wellness in my Body.
Wellness in my Home.
Wellness in my Thoughts.
Wellness in my Feelings.
Wellness in my Actions.
Wellness in my Work.
Wellness in my Leisure.
Wellness in my Dreams.
Wellness in my Soul.
Wellness in my Life.
Wellness in Relationships.
Wellness in the World.
Wellness in the Universe.

So Mote It Be.

Ritual of the Thirteenth Megaliths
Lady Janet Farrar & Lord Gavin Bone

Form:

The ritual requires thirteen people — the Master and Lady, six other women and five other men, who arrange themselves in a large circle, man and woman alternatively deosit in the order of their alloted roles.

Ritual

The Lady starts, and then continues to her left, and so on.

I am the first of the old ones.
I have seen the dawn of time, from the suns beyond our earth.
Men call me the stone goddess, old, steadfast and wise.

I am the second of the old ones.
I opened my arms to the first one, and cooled her fire with my breath.
I was the primordial movement, the first stirring of the winds.
Men call me the father of chaos.

I am the third of the old ones.
I was the waters upon the face of the two.
From my depths all life was formed.
My face was softened by the breath of the second.
Men call me Mara, the bitter one, the sea.

I am the fourth of the old ones.
I gave my warmth to the three.
From my brillance the third one was given beauty.
Men call me Sol, the sun.

I am the fifth of the old ones.
I gave my light to the darkness.
Mine are the tides to rule.
Though my brother the fourth shows greater brillance, I too have my beauty.
Men call me the virgin;
also I am named Luna, the moon.

I am the sixth of the old ones.
I ride the earth on cloven hooves,
or on the winds of night.
I am the hunter and the hunted.
Stag and horse, bird and beast are mine;
and with the aid of the fifth,

whose call all must answer,
I reproduce my kind.
Men kill in lust for me.
I am named Herne or Pan, Cernunnos or the Horned one.

I am the seventh of the old ones.
I am the floral one; all laughter and joy are mine.
With the sixth, I call all living things to join our dance.
I am the eternal She who knows not destruction.
The silver fish are mine,
as are also the spinners of webs, the weavers of dreams.
Men know me as the Mother, and call me great.

I am the eigth of the old ones.
I am a mystery, for I am my own twin.
My two faces are life and light.
Sol and the winds that cool him are both of my essence.
Men know me as the mover and fertiliser
and call me Air and Fire.

I am the ninth of the old ones.
With the eighth, I am wholeness, for I am love and law.
The father of chaos and the bitter sea are my parents.
Men know me as the nourisher and shape-giver,
and call me Water and Earth.
My brother the eighth and I are the quartered circle of creation.

I am the tenth of the old ones.
I am the pupil of all the others.
I begin with four, and then have two, and end with three.
From the belly I came, and to the womb I go.
I am nothing, yet I am Lord of all.
I shall cease, and yet return.
I am good, yet am I more terrible than those who have gone before.
I am Man.

I am the eleventh of the old ones.
I too am the pupil.
With the tenth, I seek the truth.
There is no He without She.
Mine is the great cauldron of creation, yet am I ever virgin.
I am even more terrible then the tenth,
for logic and reason are not mine
when my little ones are destroyed by any of the others.
I am warm yet cold, gentle yet destructive.
I mirror the stone one and the floral one.
I am Woman.

I am the twelfth of the old ones.
Hide from my face if you will, but know that
I am the most powerful of all.
The tenth and eleventh dance with me,
and even the floral one weeps summer tears at my command.
For I am an ever-turning wheel.
I am the spinner and the weaver,
and I also cut the silver cords of time.
Men know me as Fate,
and I am the Hermaphrodite.

I am the thirteenth of the old ones.
I am the shadow of the sanctuary, and the silver wheel.
I am feared, yet loved and often yearned for.
I ride my white mare over the battlefields,
and in my arms the sick and the tired find rest.
We shall be together many times,
for though I am the victor, yet am I also the loneliest of all the
thirteen.

To seek the twelve is to know that I am but an illusion.
Woe is to me, the thirteenth one - and yet all joy is mine also;
for from my embrace is renewed life;
and to know me is to meet, know, remember and love again.

Men know me as Death -
yet I am the comforter and renewer,
the correcting principle in creation.
The scythe and the victor's crown are mine;
for of all the thirteen,
I am the only one who is not eternal.
(Then all repeat in unison)
We are the henge of creation,
the megaliths of old,
the guardians of the path of knowledge,
the thirteen keepers of the sacred circle.

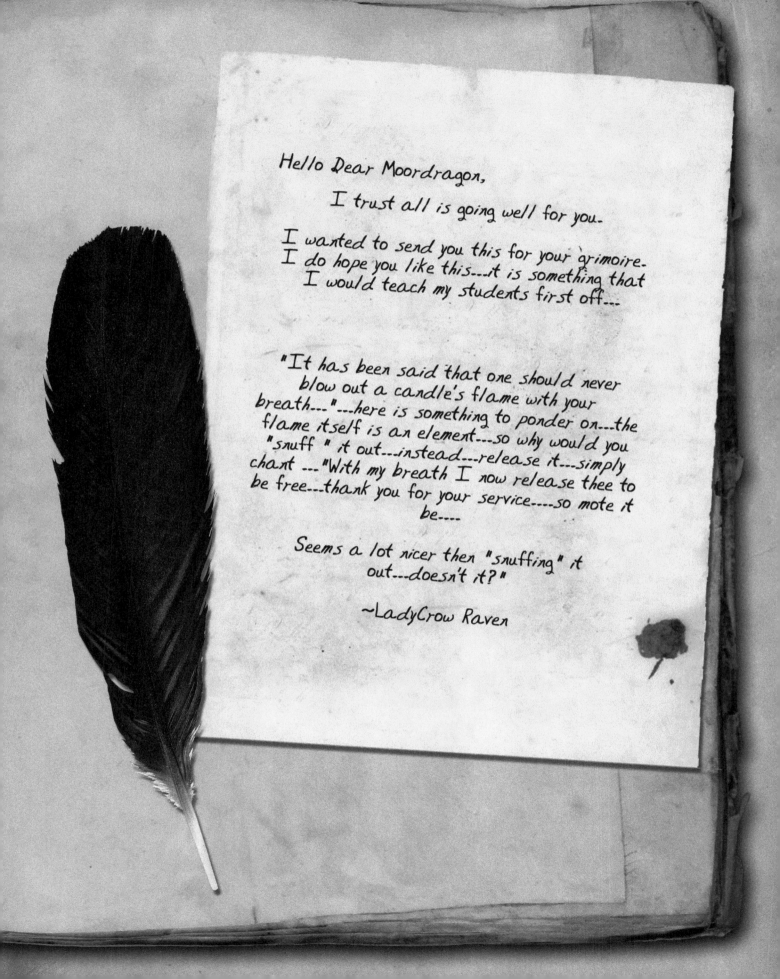

Hello Dear Moordragon,

    I trust all is going well for you.

I wanted to send you this for your grimoire.
I do hope you like this---it is something that
    I would teach my students first off---

"It has been said that one should never
  blow out a candle's flame with your
breath---"---here is something to ponder on---the
flame itself is an element---so why would you
"snuff" it out---instead---release it---simply
chant ---"With my breath I now release thee to
be free---thank you for your service----so mote it
    be----

Seems a lot nicer then "snuffing" it
    out---doesn't it?"

    ~LadyCrow Raven

THE GREAT RITE
Lord Raymond Buckland

The ancient hieros gamos, or "Sacred Marriage", was the sublime rite between priest/priestess and supplicant, representative of the union of the deities. There are many historical/mythological examples found, typical being the union between Zeus and Hera. Sacred marriage between deity and human may be seen in that between Demeter and Iasion, which took place in a thrice-plowed field. Lord James Frazer, mentions examples of marriage of the gods to the priesthood in Athens, Babylonia, Egypt and Platœa, and in Crete of a sacred marriage between a sun god and a moon goddess. In the Babylonian Akitu Festival the king, as representative of the High God, celebrates a sacred marriage with a chosen priestess. In Witchcraft many traditions have incorporated the hieros gamos under the name "Great Rite", and it is an essential part of the ritual of the Third Degree Initiation.

Many Witches have only a hazy idea of what is involved in the great Rite. There is a lot of misunderstanding, misrepresentation, and pure ignorance on the subject. Many uninformed believe it to be no more than an excuse for sex in the Sacred Circle. Others think that it is used, any and every time, to raise power for the working of magic.

Some texts state: In Witchcraft, the Great Rite is a form of sex magic that includes either ritual sexual intercourse or else a ritual symbolic representation of sexual intercourse. Most often it is performed by the High Priest and High Priestess, but other participants can be elected to perform the Rite.

The rite does take place between the Third Degree Initiate and the High Priest or High Priestess (depending upon the sex of the Initiate) conducting the elevation. It is not a matter of raising power in order to perform magic. It is a sacred blending symbolizing the ultimate union with deity. As Lord R. F. Willetts points out, this is "a part of the Oriental ritual pattern underlying the concept of such relationships as the Great Mother - Attis, Ishtar-Tammuz, Aphrodite-Adonis." In the rites of the Mysteries of Eleusis there is a sacred marriage between Hades and Persephone. Some refer to this as a union between the Hierophant (Initiate) and the Priestess, much as in the Witchcraft ritual. There is a certain similarity found in the Saora tribe of Orissa, India, where the shaman is believed to have a spiritual wife (female shamans have a spiritual husband) who, in dreams, visits and lies with the shaman. These guardian spouses give strength and inspiration to the shaman. In their minds, these nocturnal marriages are real.

There is sex involved in the Witchcraft Great Rite. Yet it is not sex for its own sake. It is a very sacred, holy union which is the culmination not only of that particular ritual but of the whole journey that the Initiate has traveled through the degrees (usually over a period of several years).

If there is a need to raise power to perform magic then there are many ways of doing this that do not involve the Great Rite and, indeed, it would be most incorrect to use that rite for such a mundane purpose.

Sex magic is one of many ways of raising power but in that instance is not done with the participants representing god or goddess nor with it being that same holy and symbolic union with deity.

In the Great Rite, the High Priest/Priestess is, of course, representing the deity. The Hierophant then becomes, briefly, the representative of the other deity for the sacred marriage. As a holy union, the rite would not normally be performed with spectators. In actual fact, however, in Witchcraft it is sometimes permissible for others who are also of that sublime degree, to be present and witness it. It is still not, even in such an instance, an excuse for an orgy of copulating couples. The sacredness and honoring of the deities is always paramount.

It is considered incorrect for the Great Rite to be performed symbolically rather than actually, unless there is some very real reason – such as a medical condition – to prevent the full practice. However, symbolic echoes of the union are found in such rituals as the Cakes & Wine (or Cakes & Ale) segments of other rites, where Priest and Priestess bring together athamé and cup to symbolize the union.

This pantomime would never be done in the Great Rite itself, however.

Journeying to the Green

by Lady Levanah Shell Bdolak

It is the day before the first eve of Spring. There is still a crisp coolness in the air but the wee flower fairies are busy painting the newly opened buds. The breath of the goddess both warms and cools the land as she turns toward the upward spiral of life.

The earth is alive. It breathes, it sighs in the wind, it is loved by the gentle rain, caressed by the young fire of the sun and charmed by the desire of the humans who await the greening. I was sitting in my garden meditating on the Equinox, the balance of the light and the dark. I was trying to prepare myself for the ritual of moving through the doorway that opens between the worlds.

I closed my eyes. Suddenly before me stood a Being of the light. It was almost six feet tall and rays of light seemed to shimmer from it as if it were a kinetic rainbow. I say "it" because it was neither significantly male nor female. It simply was and it smiled at me. It reached out it's arm to take my hand and said, "Come." I hesitated but then felt a warmth move through me. "I am your guide to take you through the threshold. But first, we must visit the ancestral spirits to get their blessings. Come. Do not be afraid."

And so I took it's hand. Suddenly around me was a mist of grey blue light like early morning fog. But instead of chilling me with a wetness it seemed to energize me with pinpoints of light.

As we walked through the thick grey-blue fog I started to realize that we were descending into the earth. With each footstep I felt pulled down into the depths of caverns of time into the origins where the first seed of light and life took hold.

The fog turned into rivulets of viscous red that thinned and ran in flowing streams around us, through us and beyond us. We were moving through the streams of life and the light of all creation. Suddenly I could see figures walking toward us. A woman moved towards me. She had long dark hair and piercing blue eyes. "I am your great-great-grandmother. I am the one you inherit your magic from. You do not remember me but I still watch over you. For me you are the child of promise. When you need help remember me." And then she faded from view as if she was never there. And then I could see a very faded yet true image of my mother. She had died four years before. She smiled a gentle sad smile and said, "Many things have come between us but remember that I love you always. Carry my love in your heart." And she too faded away. I felt sad, but yet something had resolved itself and I felt lightened, as if the burden of all the conflict with my mother had passed on; and now I could be one with the Earth Mother, for she is the true mother of us all.

The scene seemed to fade and then my guide was leading me on a path in the woods. And suddenly I could see a round cheery face. His skin was a shade of light green and something about him made me feel warm and sensual as if every part of me was alive and straining to celebrate the life I felt. He did not smile but his face was somehow a message of smile. And I could smell green, the smell of newly cut grass and the sweet pungency of leaves underfoot in the woods. You are the Green Man, I thought. He said nothing but gestured me to follow him. He turned and broke into a fast walk. Everywhere he walked the landscape turned green with grass underfoot, trees sprouting Spring leaves, masses of flowers springing up. He was the bringer of the green. Soon he picked up speed, running on and I followed in his wake breathing in the scents of his creations. Soon I could see that he was not just running but chasing a figure who had been way in front of him but now he was catching up to her. It was the Goddess of the Spring, the maiden Eostre of the early days of the growing. And the Green Man ran on, racing after the Goddess. Her hair was streaming behind her. It was blonde billowing hair in the wind, and then it was deep shining black hair and then flame blue flashing as she ran like the wind. She was naked and yet she ran so fast I could barely see her flashing naked figure. The Green Man ran after her and each place he ran past and touched turned green. Leaves sprang from trees, grass grew green under his feet, and vines sprang up quickly. Flowers bloomed and filled the air with the scent of love and lust. Suddenly the hillsides were lush with bright yellow flowers. I ran after the Green Man following in his footsteps, breathing in the pungent smells of the new Spring Air.

We came to a grove of giant tall trees that formed a circle. Here the Goddess and the Green Man stopped. I could no longer see them but I could hear them playing, laughing and making love. They were hidden from my sight and yet they seemed to be all around me filling the grove with their sounds, their passion and their lust. And the ancient whistles of the panpipes streamed through the grove.

The Grove was alive with the sounds of birds, insects, the breeze of a newly warmed Spring air and a breath of the Mother Goddess. I could hear the earth breathe as if she had awakened from a deep sleep. And then I heard a golden voice softly yet strongly speaking on the wind, "Slumber no more. Awaken to the dance of life. Celebrate with me!"

And for a moment I felt the wildness within me and I danced and spun wildly around the grove in a mad frenzy, feeling the life within me and around me til I finally collapsed on the ground, hugging the earth as I could feel its warming. The Grove was spinning with the cone of energy I had created. And the gates of the ancients were open. The old and the new were blending to usher in a new season of the light. I felt the light fill me and for a moment I could feel the kiss of the goddess on my cheek.

Be fruitful she whispered. Fill the earth with my blessings.

And then I heard my guide speak. Open your eyes it said.

For tonight is the equinox and you will celebrate the mysteries with your coven. And then it too faded away.

And so I opened my eyes. I was sitting in my chair at home in my garden. There were wee little fairies painting the budding flowers with their palette of colorful brushes. The hummingbirds were flying to the deep throated flowers and the young squirrels were running up and down the pine trees playing their own game of hide and seek. The breath of life was gaining momentum by the moment and all things green seemed to shine with a special glow of life. The turning of the wheel was coming and the season of the light was beginning to green our earth and in turn our human feelings were also opening with new essence.

She who is the light of love, compassion and wonderment and he who greens all he touches were beginning to bless us with their fruitfulness as the season shifts to the light. And so the greening had begun.

This note was found inside the back of the Grimoire.

It is a note hastily written by Moordragon while a raid by witch-hunters was in progress somewhere in the village.

It would appear that he wrote the note and buried his Grimoire in a prepared hiding place beneath his house.

The reference to "The Black Book of Lailoken" is a mystery, but apparently somewhere in the vicinity of where Mithewinter once stood, is hidden an ancient black book of some importance.

---Bob Hobbs

As I pen this message, the witch-hunters have raided Mithewinter from the far end of Westewoode. House by house, they are arresting people and setting fire to their homes. I fear that all of Mithewinter shall be razed to the ground ere this day is done. I have prepared a place to hide this Grimoire should the day come when the witch-hunters would find our sanctuary...and that day is upon us. To whomever finds this book one day, know you that a magical place once stood here. The buildings and the people may be gone, but the magic remains. I am not long for this world for the hunters will soon be upon my doorstep. Find the Black Book of Lailoken. Start with Ariel's note. It contains the clues to find it. Once found, keep it hidden...keep it locked...

Fenris MoorDragon

Rev. Kurt R. [...]
[...]tor of Zion's Evan-
[...]utheran Church

[...]story of that terrible
[...]n which struk our be-
[...]ty fifty years ago is not an
[...] task for one living half a cen-
[...]y later. It requires an eye wit-
[...]s to do it and even than one never
[...]n give an accurate account of what
[...]appened on that terrible night of
[...]e eighth of Octo[...]. I there-
[...]re do not claim to state in the fol-
[...]wing all of what happened nor do
[...]venture to be looked for as author-
[...]y of all what the following tale
[...]tains. It is in part a compilation
[...] stories told me and of what I have
[...]d concerning this horrible disast-
[...], and is given to the reader in con-
[...]ection with the fact that the [...]
[...]go fire is [...] connected with the
[...]story of [...] Lutheran Church,
[...] a matter [...] it is with the his-
[...]ory of the Congregational and Ro-
[...]an Catholic Church as well as with
[...]e city in general. the Black Order

The summer of [...] will ever be
[...]memorable [...] in Northern Wis-
[...]nsin and [...], as indeed in
[...]any other [...]ities. It will be
[...]emorable throughout the United
[...]tes for its shipwrecks, [...] the
[...]ses by fire in [...] quarter, for
[...]e crimes and [...] have
[...]st shadow [...]
[...]ut especia[...]
[...]nsin and
[...]r the un[...]
[...]ut the[...]
[...]evasta[...]
[...]nsig[...]
[...]nain [...]
[...]ires

[...]atively without snow, qui[...]
[...]ity to the lumbermen. A[...]
spring was prophecied, there[...]
unusual amount of rain. Th[...]
heavy rain had fallen on July [...]
left little trace of it. The s[...]
even were so dry that [...] coul[...]
over the surface. The want o[...]
was [...] The Ninth Circle [...]
Railroad was then just buildin[...]
Northern extension from Fort[...]
and (Green Bay) to Menu[...]
[...]. Many of the railroad [...]
laid down their tools and refus[...]
work owing to the insuff[...]
amount of drinking water and [...]
reported that the [...] Co. h[...]
gang of men carr[...] water[...]
the tracks many [...]. The [...]
ported rain [...]
but did not leav[...]
Forest fires were [...]
Pensaukee, Litt[...]
and across the [...]
and vicinity. [...]
constantly fight[...]
least a month, [...]
the devouring. [...]
Bay Advocate" [...]
gate the followin[...]
tigo the house [...]
Berner and [...]
ter are reported [...]
paper we find [...]
account of a battle [...]
at Peshtigo on Sunday [...]
24th, just two weeks [...]
struction of the villa[...]

Sabbath, the 24th wa[...] exce[...]
a fearful time in [...]. For
eral days the fires [...] n r[...]
in the timbers near [...] O[...]
and the north and e[...] of us. F[...]
the fire was raging a few miles
of the village, Saturday it [...]
through to the river about [...]
above town, and Saturday n[...]
much danger was apprehended [...]
the sparks and cinders that [...]
[...] th[...] nt the [...]

CPSIA information can be obtained
at www.ICGtesting.com
Printed in the USA
FSHW011546050419
56949FS